ONE NIGHT IN MISSISSIPPI

ONE NIGHT IN MISSISSIPPI

A NOVEL

CRAIG SHREVE

TAP
BOOKS

This is a work of fiction. Any resemblance to real persons or real events — with the exception of references to historical figures and events that are now part of the public record — is purely coincidental.

Editor: Diane Young
Design: Laura Boyle
Printer: Webcom
Cover Design: Laura Boyle
Image credits: Oriontrail/istockphoto.com

Library and Archives Canada Cataloguing in Publication

Shreve, Craig, author
     One night in Mississippi / Craig Shreve.
Issued in print and electronic formats.

ISBN 978-1-4597-3099-1 (pbk.).--ISBN 978-1-4597-3100-4 (pdf).-- ISBN 978-1-4597-3101-1 (epub)

     I. Title.
PS8637.H735O54 2015   C813'.6   C2014-906617-1
                                    C2014-906618-X

1   2   3   4   5   19   18   17   16   15

Conseil des Arts du Canada   Canada Council for the Arts   Canadä   ONTARIO ARTS COUNCIL
CONSEIL DES ARTS DE L'ONTARIO
an Ontario government agency
un organisme du gouvernement de l'Ontario

We acknowledge the support of the **Canada Council for the Arts** and the **Ontario Arts Council** for our publishing program. We also acknowledge the financial support of the **Government of Canada** through the **Canada Book Fund** and **Livres Canada Books,** and the **Government of Ontario** through the **Ontario Book Publishing Tax Credit** and the **Ontario Media Development Corporation**.

Care has been taken to trace the ownership of copyright material used in this book. The author and the publisher welcome any information enabling them to rectify any references or credits in subsequent editions.

J. Kirk Howard, President

Printed and bound in Canada.

VISIT US AT
www.dundurn.com/TAPbooks

TAP Books Ltd.
3 Church Street, Suite 500
Toronto, Ontario, Canada
M5E 1M2

When you are in Mississippi, the rest of America doesn't seem real; and when you are in the rest of America, Mississippi doesn't seem real.

– *Robert "Bob" Moses*

PROLOGUE

THE BOY WE TOOK wasn't much older than I was. Eighteen, maybe nineteen. At the time, I couldn't even say for sure what we were doing or why we were forcing him to get into the car. He was just standing by the side of the road when we found him and he told us he was out looking for his brother. Uncle Patrick had said he was a troublemaker, and I didn't question it. Didn't question any of it, really. Don't think things would have been much different if I had. Things would have happened exactly the way they happened, except maybe I wouldn't have been a part of it. They certainly wouldn't have been any different for the boy in the back seat of Uncle Patrick's Studebaker.

My father was in another car that had already driven up ahead. I was sandwiched in the front seat between my uncle and another man I'd just met a few hours earlier. The boy sat behind us, alone. Uncle Patrick nudged me.

"You all right, Earl?"

"Yeah," I replied. "I'm OK."

I looked in the rear-view mirror. The boy was quiet, gazing out the window as we drove. I wished I was somewhere else, and I'm sure he did as well, but it was too late now, for both of us. He knew what was coming as well as I did. We were two boys who had played at being men, and we were on our way to pay the price.

WARREN

1

MISSISSIPPI, 1965

WE HAD INTENDED to lay my brother to rest on Sunday, but we had to postpone our plans while we waited for the body. The authorities had said they would need a week for the autopsy, and that the body would be delivered to the family at that time, but seven days stretched to ten before Graden was finally brought home to the farm for burial.

During the wait there had been no message from the sheriff or the medical office, and when two men showed up and unloaded the corpse from the back of their pickup, there was no apology either. Graden's body was wrapped in a green tarp bundled with twine. The men laid it on the front porch and asked my father to sign for it as if it were a package he had ordered from a department store catalogue and told him that both the tarp and twine would have to be returned. My father's face was impassive, but his hand shook slightly when he reached for the pen. He couldn't read, but he took a few moments to look over the sheet anyway before scratching his name.

I watched from the side of the house as the men drove away. There was no laneway — the area surrounding the house was devoid of grass, although weeds somehow managed to flourish. My sisters, Glenda and Etta, would pick the weeds once a week as well as collect fallen pecans from the tree by the front porch. Then they would sweep the entire area with coarse brooms, keeping the dirt lawn as immaculate as any green one. Swirls of dust kicked up behind the truck's tires, partially obscuring it as it headed off down the dusty red road into town. The edges of the pickup shimmered liquidly in the heat, a child's picture coloured outside the lines.

I dipped a bucket into the well and took a long, cool drink. I dipped the bucket a second time, splashed water onto my hands and face, and then went into the house to put on my church clothes.

◄ ►

The lot was not a large one, but it belonged to us, and that in itself was significant. My father had bought the house and the farm from a white store owner for three hundred dollars — all the money that he had managed to save during long, hard years as a tenant farmer. The work had marked him. His face was dark and wrinkled, the skin on his arms was papery thin, revealing the tendons and ropy muscles underneath, and the knuckles on his hands were so swollen that he couldn't close them into a fist. Still, I had never heard him complain. It was a proud day for any black man in Mississippi to come to own a piece of land, and he had probably never dreamed that he would someday have to bury his son on it.

Pastor Lonny and a few family members had arrived the night before the originally planned funeral day, and my father had to find space for them during the delay. The house was not very big to begin with, just a wooden shack set up on cinder blocks with a small porch in the front and a set of steps in the back. In some spots there were spaces between the floorboards large enough that you could see the ground underneath, and when it stormed, the boards lifted and bowed, and sometimes had to be hammered back in place after the storm had passed There was a narrow hallway with two rooms on either side, each square and plain with a single window. On one side of the house were my parents' room and a kitchen; on the other side, one bedroom for Graden and me and another for Glenda and Etta.

When Pastor Lonny arrived, he was given our room. The women were split among my parents' and sisters' rooms, so during the three-day wait Graden and I, two uncles, and eight cousins were relegated to sleeping on the floor of the kitchen and the hallway, our bodies locked together in the cramped space like jigsaw pieces. On the third night I was overcome by the heat of too many bodies. I took my blanket and picked my way through the maze of legs and arms out to the porch. Glenda and Etta were already there, perched on the top step.

Etta looked up at me.

"Can't sleep?"

"Too damn hot," I said sitting next to her. "And Uncle Jerry snores."

"So does his wife."

She rolled her eyes and nudged her shoulder into me. The crickets that usually filled the night were mostly silent, and the three of us sat there, huddled in our blankets in the dark until Etta spoke again.

"I just want this to be over. They always take the best of us."

Glenda tightened her blanket around her neck and stood abruptly, walking back inside without looking at me.

"I'm sorry," Etta said. "I didn't mean nothing by it. Don't let her bother you."

"It's all right. Can't be hurt by what's true."

She put her hand on mine.

"Warren, he was bent on this. There wasn't anything to be done."

I said nothing, and she let it go. We cooled ourselves in the night air before picking our way back inside to lie down among the mass of bodies, she in her room and I on the hallway floor.

After the truck delivered my brother's body and drove away, the family gathered at the southeast corner of the yard where my father had dug the grave. He had hit hard-packed clay about four feet down and had to settle for that depth. I had sat in the backyard at times and watched him, unable to hold a shovel with my crippled right hand, a painful reminder of my place bestowed on me by a grease-slick white boy during one of my rare visits into town. The doctor had to sever the ring and pinky fingers just ahead of the second knuckle, leaving useless, wiggling nubs. The middle and index fingers were curved inwards towards the palm, the tendons too damaged to stretch them straight. The entire hand was withered, the palm and the back dark with scar tissue.

I was unable to help my father in any way other than to bring him water and the occasional piece of bread or cured meat, which he accepted in silence, not looking at me. Other times, I simply couldn't watch and had to go back to the house.

The head of the grave was marked with a plain wooden cross, and Pastor Lonny stood beside it as he delivered his eulogy. I heard very little of it. I stood off to the side, away from the rest of the family, and stared off over the pastor's shoulder. Rows of cotton trailed out behind him, blooming white tufts speared on cracked and drying twigs. Beyond that, a small patch of peanut plants, then the woods, thick patches of pine and oak and chestnut. There were deer in the woods as well, feeding on wild oats and peas, and in the dense underbrush, the occasional sign of trails left behind by the Indians who had hunted them.

I looked around the makeshift congregation, who were turned towards the pastor, their heads bowed. A rare breeze drifted across the yard, bringing with it the faint but undeniable stench of filth from the outhouse, but if anyone noticed, they gave no sign. The pastor continued, "A young man of passion, of vision, of commitment. One of our brightest lights snuffed out far too soon, and all our lives are a darker place for it. But if each of us keeps but a piece of his memory alive, then we also keep a piece of that light alive."

The breeze died as suddenly as it had come up, and the stifling heat reclaimed the now-still air. Tiny black gnats resumed their buzzing around the sweat-soaked necks and faces. No hand was waved to deter them.

When the pastor had finished, he nodded at my father. The coffin was a simple pine box that he had built, with four makeshift handles. There was nothing to put inside as a cushion, and I thought I heard my brother's remains bump against the side as my father and my uncles lowered the box into the shallow grave. I stared at my father with a sudden and unreasonable anger, but he returned my look with an expression so fierce it made mine seem pale. Pastor Lonny offered a final benediction, my mother dropped a single flower atop the pine coffin, and the ceremony was closed with a moment of silence.

I bowed my head, but my jaw was clenched. I had ignored most of the eulogy, but I didn't have to hear it to know that it was a long, drawn-out, and overly dramatic summary of how Graden had lived, with not one word about how he had died. Just as there hadn't been one word said about it among ourselves in the months since he had first gone missing. Papa had kept working the field, Mama had kept tending the kitchen, and Etta and Glenda had kept doing their chores. Everyone had carried on, but no one had talked about it. We had turned inward when we most needed to come together, and no one more so than I.

Anger swelled up inside me, and I understood that it was Graden's anger that I felt. I remembered a day when Mama had taken Graden with her while she went to do some cooking and cleaning for a white family. I was out in the field when they returned, and when I walked into the house, Graden was standing in the hallway looking at the floor.

"What's wrong with you?" I asked.

He was only seven at the time, but when he lifted his head, the expression on his face frightened me. He was enraged.

"We got holes in our floor."

"Be glad we got a floor," I said. I was hoping he would laugh, but he didn't.

"White folks don't have holes in their floors. They got shiny floors and bright walls and big windows."

"If you start thinking about all the things that some folks have that we don't, you're gonna be standing there for a long time."

He continued on as if I hadn't even spoken. His eyes were fiery.

"Papa always braggin' about how hard he worked to buy this place, but it ain't nothing but a pile of sticks."

I grabbed him by the shoulders and steered him outside, turning my head quickly to make sure no one else was nearby.

"You better not ever let Mama or Papa hear you talking like that."

"Why? It's true. What's wrong with saying what's true?"

"Maybe it is. But true or not, ain't no sense in saying something that you can't do anything about."

He shrugged my hands off him and walked away. I never forgot Graden's expression that day. It was my brother who saw more clearly than any of us the hypocrisy and hopelessness that we swallowed like candied treats. It was Graden who tried to convince us that we should want more, that we could be more. It was Graden who took a stand, time and time again, even when the people around him begged him not to. It was Graden who took a stand and hoped that I would stand with him.

I spat on the ground, then remembering where I was, looked up to make sure I had not been seen. No one moved. If they heard me at all, they reacted the same way they did to the gnats buzzing around them, to the injustice of Graden's murder, and to every oppressive act and action that kept them from ever rising above a station that they meekly accepted as their own.

They did nothing.

2

DETROIT, 2008

I OPENED THE DOOR and entered the near-empty apartment. One brown-cushioned chair and one loveseat. One leather recliner, the arms torn and rupturing foam. A wrought-iron coffee table set between them. The same mismatched furniture that was here when I moved in three years ago. The walls were bare, smudged, and yellowing. The water-stained ceiling shed occasional paint flakes onto the loosening curls of the carpet, and when the couple in the apartment above fought or fucked, the living room took on the feel of a lightly shaken snow-globe.

These were the places I had lived in since leaving Mississippi: A wooden lodge on an abandoned lot in rural Tennessee; an attic above a flower shop down the street from my sister's house in Philadelphia; a mould-infested hostel that slept eight to a room off the campus of Loyola University.

I'd dropped out of college with one semester remaining, because graduating from college was Graden's dream and I didn't feel I should be the one to achieve it. If I'd stayed, I could have been an engineer. Instead I took work cleaning out horse stalls on a farm in Kentucky. I worked on a dock in Maine, gutting fish. I loaded railway cars. I worked in lumberyards and on road crews and in a leather tannery. Once, I apprenticed for a cabinet maker, but the work was too fine for my crippled hand. I would trace the old man's curls and grooves with my fingers, the wood sometimes still warm from the cutting, wistfully admiring the detail, but I could never match the work myself.

I drifted with no destination and no desire to stay in any one place. As a boy growing up in Mississippi, I had always planned on taking over the farm from Pa and raising my own family there. I'd never expected to leave the county, much less the state, but after Graden's death I had run so far that I had seen near half the country before I found a purpose again.

The cabinet maker kept a small television in his shop so he could watch baseball games while he worked, and it was there that I saw the news that would shape the rest of my life. Images of a soft-jowled man, close-cropped hair starting far back on his forehead, heavy glasses. I sat in a chair, broom in hand, and listened to the newsman detail the conviction of Byron De La Beckwith, twice let go on charges in the 1963 murder of NAACP activist Medgar Evers, but now convicted, thirty-one years later. They walked him down the steps of the courthouse while crowds shouted, jubilant on one side of the steps and outraged on the other.

I remembered gathering on the steps of a similar court-house in Jackson, watching eight men walk free after the charges against them were thrown out. There hadn't even been a trial for Graden. The judge heard the charges and the evidence, dismissed them, and after months of waiting, the whole thing was over in the space of a few minutes.

The cabinet maker appeared in the doorway. I'd never told him or anyone else about my brother, but he must have seen something in my face while I sat in front of the television, because he simply nodded at me and took the broom from my hand.

"It's all right," he said. "Go home."

I stayed up all night, watching the news coverage. Experts debated the right and wrong of the conviction while the same footage looped through, over and over, but all I could think about was standing on those courthouse steps so many years ago, helpless.

I started to gather every piece of information I could about my brother's case. I kept a folder with articles, notes, names, and dates. I obtained a copy of the autopsy report. I never went back to the cabinet maker's shop, but I think he expected as much when he sent me home. I was restless. I was fifty-four years old when I saw De La Beckwith convicted. I had wasted so much time, and now I couldn't sit still.

At the end of each work day I would return to whatever place I had found at the time, aching and often dirty, and start carefully writing out letters to lawyers and politicians. I kept it all to myself at first, but I needed a permanent address where I could receive responses, so I called Etta, who now lived in Philadelphia. She agreed, and I made daily visits to post offices, hoping for a packet of forwarded mail from her. At first all I received were a few vague, noncommittal replies. I wrote letters to the FBI and to the Justice Department, and they responded with form letters assuring me they would look at the case, but carefully explaining how backlogged they were.

Yet they continued to pursue convictions. In 2001, Thomas E. Blanton, Jr. was sentenced for his role in the 1963 bombing of the Sixteenth Street Baptist Church in Birmingham, a blast that had killed four young girls who were inside preparing for a sermon to be titled "The Love That Forgives." In 2005, Edgar Ray Killen was found guilty of three counts of murder in the 1964 slaying of civil rights workers James Chaney, Andrew Goodman, and Michael Schwerner in Mississippi. He received three consecutive twenty-year sentences. He was eighty years old.

I expanded my letter-writing campaign to include newspapers and television stations, and that's when things took off. Etta was swamped with mail, and I received new packages from her almost every day. The official agencies were still cautious in their responses, but the reaction of the media and the public was overwhelming. I began to give interviews.

My elder sister, Glenda, called from Baltimore, where she had settled to be close to the nursing home where our mother lived.

"Mama and I saw you on the news today. You know she's not well."

"How is she?"

"She's not well, I just told you. Then she sees all this stuff about Graden on the news all over again. It's not good for her."

"Then why are you letting her watch it?"

"Don't do that. Don't you talk to me about taking care of Mama! I'm the one that's here. Do you even care?"

Glenda raged at me for stirring things up, but I doubted that I was having the impact on our mother that she claimed. I had visited Ma a few times, and although there was the occasional spark of recognition, more often there was just a confused stare. Once, when I was standing in the doorway with the sunlight streaming in from the hallway window behind me, she smiled wistfully and called me "Graden." I allowed her a moment of illusion, then backed out of the room and left the home. I never went back.

While Glenda shouted at me through the phone, I listened quietly, having no justification to offer her.

After a while Etta set up an email address for me, although I had no idea how to use it. She sent me printouts of the messages at first, but as they started to come in greater numbers, she insisted that I learn. And so I did. I received messages of support from blacks and whites alike, and I received messages of hatred from blacks and whites alike. I didn't find the former encouraging or the latter troubling. There were eight men's names in my folder, and one by one they were found. Six were still alive.

Daniel Olsen was the first. A television reporter from a local station tracked him to a run-down trailer park outside of Mobile, Alabama. The station paid to fly me in for the arrest. The last time I'd seen him, he'd been at the back of the group walking down the courthouse steps. His son, Earl, who'd been charged as a minor, was beside him. Daniel had his hand on the back of his son's head, and neither of them looked up. They didn't smile and wave like the others, and they weren't dressed like them either. The six men in front of them were wearing expensive suits and ties and polished shoes. The Olsens were dressed shabbily by comparison, in plain brown shoes with simple pants and starched white shirts.

I stood on Daniel's front lawn with a cluster of news cameras behind me. The driveway was cracked, and the pieces of pavement jutted up against each other like ice floes. The lawn was littered with small clay pots, some holding plants, others seemingly just filled with dirt. Grass was sparse. Neighbours opened their trailer doors to watch, standing half-in, half-out, gawking at the crowd approaching Daniel's front step, but ready in a moment to duck back into safety. I stayed back while they knocked. When Daniel answered the door, he seemed bewildered at the sight of the cameras and the officers. He was wearing pyjama bottoms and slippers, and the few strands of white hair that remained flicked above his head in the wind. I could hear the TV playing behind him, but I couldn't make out the show. An officer read the charges and handcuffed him on the front step. I heard one of the reporters say Graden's name, but instead of clarifying things, the name only seemed to confuse him further. The reporter got close enough to push a microphone towards him.

"Do you recognize this man?"

The reporter tipped his head in my direction. Daniel turned towards me, but there was no visible response, and an officer shoved the reporter away.

When they put Daniel in the back of the cruiser, he still wore the same lost look that he'd had when they knocked. He said nothing except to ask if he could go back inside to get a shirt.

"How do you feel?" Etta asked me that night on the phone.

"I don't know," I replied, and it was the truth. I had difficulty connecting the helpless old man who had been led away to prison to the younger version of himself whom I'd last seen striding down the steps of that Mississippi courthouse.

"What about you?"

"I don't know either," she said. "In truth, I don't feel like it changes anything. But I know that this means more to you. I know it's … something different for you."

I let that hang on the line between us and was grateful that she didn't continue. It was true that I had hoped for more. I felt as uncertain as Daniel had looked, but I had started and I intended to keep going.

None of them were difficult to find, because none of them were hiding. Daniel's brother, Patrick Olsen, was still in Mississippi. His son, Earl Olsen, was deceased. Rob Tywater and his cousin Barry were in Georgia. Blaine Pimpton was in Seattle, Paul Poust was in South Carolina, and Marty Bavon was also deceased.

I was there for every one of the arrests. I never went to any of the trials — I couldn't stand to hear the details again, to hear the arguments of the defence, to risk having to stand on another set of courthouse steps if one of them were set free — but I was always there for the arrests. I looked at their faces and registered the stages. First shock, then disorientation, then indignant anger, turning, each one of them, to the camera to either shout or mutter some variation of "That all happened a long time ago …"

It never seemed long ago to me. Standing in the living room of my apartment in Detroit, it was still as fresh for me as it had been that summer in Mississippi.

Still wearing my coat, I walked into the kitchen to start the kettle.

I checked the cupboards. Just a few pots and pans, nothing I couldn't leave behind. I went to the bedroom, opened the closets, then the bathroom, where I had left a half-bottle of aspirin and some eye drops in the cabinet. I put them in my coat pocket, then closed the cabinet and went back to the kitchen to fix my coffee.

The call had come two weeks ago as an anonymous tip, left after I had been featured on a national news special. Someone thought that they recognized a man in the picture. Earl Olsen. Etta warned me that the caller could be a crank. We'd had plenty of bogus tipsters over the years, but I checked into every one of them, no matter how far-fetched they seemed. Earl's father had told investigators years ago that his son was dead, but after the call, I got in touch with the coroner's office and the Jackson county police department. Neither had a death certificate or any official record. The official I spoke to confessed that records older than ten years were spotty at best. The sheriff's office had moved in 1973 and several boxes were lost. Records didn't go electronic until 1997 and it wasn't until 2001 that all of the old records had been completed. I had to know.

I poured the coffee into a thermos. I dropped the aspirin and eye drops into a suitcase on the table and closed it. Everything else I owned was already in a duffel bag in the backseat of the rented Explorer that was parked outside. I left an envelope on the table with the key to the apartment and enough cash to cover two months' rent, then I picked up the suitcase and the thermos and walked out.

◄ 3 ►

MISSISSIPPI, 1946

MY MOTHER SPENT thirteen hours in labour, sweating and screaming in my parents' bedroom with Aunt Louise at her side. The radio was on, tuned in to the country station because that was the only station we could pick up and at that not very well. Hank Williams's voice scratched and warbled through the static, but it couldn't drown out the sounds.

I went back and forth to the kitchen, bringing buckets of water from the well, which our father would pour into a pot and heat over the stove, or else fetching a fresh blanket when the one our mother covered herself with had soaked through to the point that it needed to be rinsed out and hung from the clothesline in the backyard.

The rest of the time I sat on the porch, staring out past the thin red line of the county road and into the stand of pine trees in the distance beyond. Glenda and Etta had been sent off to a neighbour's house during the birth. Though Glenda was a year older than me — seven to my six — Papa apparently thought that seeing Mama in pain was OK for me, but not for my sisters. I didn't remember Etta's birth, don't know if I was there or not, but this time around I was present and I prayed hard. I prayed for a boy, because then he would be able to help in the fields in a few years' time, unlike my sisters who were mostly given just house and yard work as chores. I went through names in my head, weighing each one, and in the end, I decided on Henry. I hoped it was a boy, and that they named him Henry. I got half my wish.

Aunt Louise guessed that Graden must have been near ten pounds at birth. He was big to begin with and he kept growing at an impressive rate, leading Ma to sometimes chide that he was "too slow being born and too fast growing up." I'd prayed for a brother who could help in the fields, and I got more than I could have expected. By the time Graden was eight, he could pull as much cotton in a day as I could, though still not as much as Papa. By the time he was twelve, I had a hard time matching him. Walking in the row beside him, we would sometimes talk, sometimes sing, but even when we were silent I could see his lips move. I asked him one time what he was doing.

"Lessons," he replied.

"Lessons?"

"Yeah. I'm trying to memorize all the states."

"What for? You ain't ever going to leave this one."

"You don't know that."

"Do too. This is where your family is. You got a head full of stuff that you don't need."

He didn't look up, just kept trudging along, working his fingers through the bolls, and depositing the cotton in his sack. He was silent for a few steps, and when he did continue to speak, it was with his head down, as if he didn't want me to hear the words coming out of his mouth.

"You know there's places up north where black men have jobs. They get dressed up and go to work and get paid, just like white folks."

"There's places like that right here in Mississippi. It don't mean nothing to you though."

"Maybe it does."

"Now hold on. All that schooling's messing you up. Papa gets paid. How you think he bought this patch of land? People get rich off cotton."

"*We* don't. If you hadn't dropped out of school, you might have learned that."

I stopped to argue, but Graden just kept picking, and I had to bend back to my work to try to keep pace.

The next morning, Graden was not at breakfast. Mama asked if any of us had seen him. The girls both said no, but Etta fidgeted nervously. Papa looked up from his plate and fixed me with a stare.

"We got a lot of work to do today. If your brother ain't around, it's going to be a long day."

A long day in Papa's mind meant working well into the night. He finished his breakfast and walked out the back without saying another word. Mama cleared his plate, and Glenda got up to help her. When Mama's back was turned, Etta shovelled a few bites of potatoes and a piece of bread into a napkin and quickly wrapped it beneath the table. When she saw that I had noticed, she gave me a look like a puppy begging for table scraps.

I didn't say anything. She walked out to the front where I knew Graden would be hiding beneath the porch, waiting for the house to empty so that he could dash unnoticed to the road and off to school. Etta came back into the house without the napkin. She gave me a shrug and made a childlike effort at an innocent face, then continued to help Mama with the dishes.

When Graden returned home that afternoon, he changed his clothes and came out to help in the fields, and when the work was done, I could hear the paddling he took from Papa in our parents' bedroom. He limped into our room with tears on his cheeks, but I had no sympathy for him.

"Serves you right. You know I had to work twice as hard while you were running off."

Graden lay face down on his bed. "School's important."

"Not getting whipped by Papa, that's important. What are you learning that's worth that?"

"I could show you. I can teach you, if you want."

"Don't need you teaching me anything. I'm not the dumb one." I rolled over and went to sleep.

It was not the last time that Graden skipped field work in favour of school, far from it. Despite my protests, and Papa's whippings, he continued to do so any time that he felt he was falling behind in class. Rather than deter him, the punishments only seemed to strengthen his resolve. Papa had not gone to school past fourth grade, and Graden endured each whipping with a sorrow not for himself, but for our father's lack of understanding. Each time he returned to the room sorer than the time before, and each time he offered to teach me. I had only lasted in school to the eighth grade myself, and even at that I hadn't put in much effort. As the eldest son, I had set myself to farming and hadn't looked back. I refused Graden's offer of lessons each time he made it, but I was beginning to grow curious about what was in those books that made him willing to endure so much pain.

Skipping field work wasn't the only trouble that Graden got into as a boy. He was always getting caught sneaking bits of food to the mule or, when we could afford one, to the pig, or sometimes even to the foxes and coyotes that crept as far as the edge of the bush.

More than once Papa admonished him. "Them animals is good for two things — eating and working."

Each time he was caught, Graden would find his portion of dinner to be a little smaller than everyone else's, but he never let that discourage him. One day he found a crow with a broken wing behind the barn, and when he brought it to the house, Papa took one glance and told him it was going to die. Graden stubbornly went to work on nursing it back to health.

He built a makeshift heater — an old cigarette tin set over a low-burning lamp. He tied the bird's wing against its body with twine, lined the tin with wild grass, and set the bird within it. He fed it kernels of corn and bits of bread, read to it, and hid it under his bed when he left the room, knowing that if our father found out, he would be annoyed that Graden was wasting food and lamp oil. I made fun of him, told him that when his pet crow was healthy maybe he could get on its back and fly away to all those other states he had memorized, or that maybe when it died Mama would cook it in a stew or a pie, but my teasing never drew a response.

Papa was right, of course. The bird only survived for two days. I came into the room one night and found it still and stiff in the nest he had crafted for it. Pressing its wing between my fingers, I could feel that the feathers had already turned coarse and brittle. Seeing it lying there, fragile and useless, I was angry at Graden. Angry at him for sneaking off to school while Papa and I worked. Angry at him for his big words and big ideas, and for the way he seemed to feel sorry for us if we didn't agree with them. Most of all I was angry at him for wasting time on this stupid little bird. There were flocks of birds around the farm all the time, and there was nothing special about this one except that it had been foolish enough to crash into the barn and break its wing. And Graden had been foolish enough to give a damn. I decided to teach him a lesson. I poked my head out into the hallway.

"You almost ready for bed?"

"Yep," he called back from the kitchen. "I'm just helping Etta with something. I'll be right in."

"All right then. I'm tired. I'm gonna put the light out."

I didn't want to touch the bird again, but I cupped it in my hands and lifted it out of its tin. I laid it carefully inside Graden's pillow case, then brushed away a few stray blades of grass that had stuck to the dead crow's body. I changed quickly and put out the light, then crawled into bed. It wasn't long before I heard him crack open the bedroom door.

"You awake?" he whispered.

I pretended to sleep. He hesitated, then came in and closed the door behind him. I heard him scuffling about the room as he looked for his bedclothes and changed in darkness.

I stared up at the ceiling waiting for a screech or a cry, but there was neither. He must not have noticed it at first. He lay down for a bit, and I could hear him shifting to get comfortable. It was only after several turns that he made a throttled, hiccupping sound. I could just make out his form, sitting upright and patting his pillow.

"What is it?" I whispered.

I waited for his reaction, ready to mock him and his stupid bird, ready to tell him to get his head down out of the clouds.

Instead of answering me, he climbed out of bed. I heard the same scuffling sounds as he got dressed and, when I squinted in the darkness, I could see that he had kneeled down. I couldn't clearly make out what he was doing, but he appeared to be patting the floor. I heard a scraping noise and realized he was looking for the cigarette tin. The bedroom door cracked open, and he tiptoed outside.

I waited a few moments, then grabbed a shirt, and followed him. The backyard was bathed in bright moonlight. In the far corner, I could see Graden on his knees on the ground, digging a hole with his hands.

"What are you doing?"

"Burying it," he replied.

"It's just a bird. Leave it."

He turned to look at me, standing on the porch. I expected anger from him, but there was none, and the anger I had felt earlier seemed suddenly far away.

"I'm … sorry. It was me."

The words felt stupid coming out of my mouth. Who else would it have been? He turned away and continued digging.

"I didn't kill the bird, though."

"I know."

The disappointment in his voice was clear. I would have preferred his anger. There was nothing more to say. I left the porch and went to kneel down beside him, wordlessly pushing aside handfuls of dirt. After laying the bird to rest, Graden delivered a short prayer. When we returned to our bedroom, it wasn't Graden who cried, but me. It was the first time that I broke my brother's heart, but it wouldn't be the last or the most painful.

4

ONTARIO, 2008

THE GUARD AT THE BORDER told me that I would know how far north I had driven by the size of the animals on the roadside signs. I had never liked highway driving, and I was in no hurry to reach my destination. I stuck to regional roads. My route took me east first, through small towns straddling the Thames River, its surface a jumble of cracked ice. There were yellow diamond-shaped signs warning drivers to watch for ducks crossing.

When I did merge onto the 401, the yellow signs changed to deer. I drove past towns with European names — Dresden, London, Paris. I spotted one deer, chewing grass at the edge of a copse of trees, but it looked uninterested in testing the road.

By the time I reached Hamilton, I was tiring. I pulled off at a truck stop that sold T-shirts and stuffed beavers and offered the use of shower stalls. I ordered smothered chicken and ate in silence in a corner booth. It had started to snow. The men there were mostly what I thought they would be — gruff and weary and alone, sitting each at their separate tables with their heads hung over their meals. I stayed for coffee, then checked into a hotel a little farther down the road. I paid upfront so that I could be off early in the morning.

Past Toronto, the route turned north. After a hundred miles or so, the highway narrowed from six lanes to two, the radio stations switched from rock to mostly country, and the bill-boards began advertising snowmobiles, ATVs, and small boats instead of cars and trucks. I passed an eighteen-wheeler over-turned in the ditch, its trailer ruptured, its back wheels still spin-ning slowly in the wind like the legs of a turtle on its back.

The highway was exposed on both sides, and the wind whipped snow from the fields across it in thick sheets. I pushed on through Barrie and Orillia. The warning signs changed from deer to moose, and I knew I must be getting close. I slowed cross-ing a bridge to look at the shacks set up on the lake by ice-fish-ermen, so many that it looked like a village. The car slid beneath me, but not dangerously so.

When I finally reached my exit, the snow had stopped, but enough had accumulated that the words on the sign were obscured, and I had to look closely. I entered the town of Amblan, then pulled off to the side of the road to check my directions. Etta had arranged for a room for me, even though she hadn't wanted me to go.

It was Etta who had tried to bring me back into the family. Shortly after Graden's funeral, I'd left Mississippi. I was twenty-five and out on my own for the first time in my life. I made my way north slowly, going as far as I could with the money I had, then settling in a place just long enough to earn what I needed in order to move on, travelling sometimes by bus but more often in the back of a truck. In Chicago I met a school teacher who suffered from a mild palsy. I cooked and cleaned and ran his errands, and in return he let me have the apartment in the base-ment of his house. He began teaching me history and literature and science in the evenings. I earned my high school diploma at the age of twenty-nine and was accepted at Loyola University. The old man passed shortly before classes began and I struggled, but continued. It was the only way I knew.

Eventually, the man's daughter came from Washington to claim the property, and I moved into a hostel. I hadn't spoken to or heard from my own family in four years, but in my second year I found a postcard in my campus mailbox. It was from Philadelphia. The picture on the front showed the Liberty Bell, reflecting the colours of sunset. The note on the back was brief.

> *Am married now and living in Philadelphia. I tried*
> *to invite you to the wedding but had considerable dif-*
> *ficulty finding you. I was excited to hear you are in*
> *college! You have been hard on yourself. Much time*
> *has passed. I hope you are well, and I hope you find*
> *your way to visit us. Love, Etta.*

A few simple words wiped away the years and distance, but only for a short time. After rereading the postcard several times, I began to take note of the things not written. "*I was excited to hear you are in college!*" "I" not "we." No mention of the rest of the family sending their regards or of being missed. Etta had scribbled her address and phone number in a corner. I didn't reply, but I kept the card. It took the better part of a year before I finally called her.

The first visit was brief. I stayed only four days, meeting her husband and her two-year-old daughter. They welcomed me warmly, but I spoke little. Neither of my sisters had been beauti-ful, but Etta had grown into an understated elegance that made people look past her features. She was educated and cultured, but still occasionally revealed her roots with a country phrase that brought disapproving looks from her husband. I stayed in their house as a stranger. I left from there for Kentucky, knowing her less than when I'd arrived, but I wrote to her nonetheless and with the safety of several states between us, I opened up.

When I eventually moved to Philadelphia, into an apartment above a flower shop, I thought that I might have found a place to settle. It was the spring of 1980, and I was a forty-year-old man who had not planted solid roots anywhere. I began eating supper with Etta and her family two nights a week and accompanying them to church on Sundays. Gradually, I became friendly with the shop owner, who would give me my pick of the flowers that he couldn't sell. I brought them to Etta on each visit — lilacs that were cut too short, tulips whose petals drooped slightly, blooms with tiny flaws that were otherwise unapparent, picked up by the shop owner's trained eye.

We rarely talked with each other about family. Etta kept in constant touch with Mama and Glenda, and whenever the subject did come up, she would reel off updates about their lives while I sat and listened in silence. They knew that I was living nearby, but if they ever asked about me while they were talking to Etta, she never mentioned it.

Sitting on Etta's porch one night, sipping lemonade and looking out over the front yard, I was reminded of the night before Graden's body was brought home, both of us sleepless and sitting out in front of our old place in Mississippi.

"I wish I could have been at Papa's funeral."

"We couldn't find you. I tried, but that was before I was able to track you down."

"Thing is, I never was trying to hide. Just didn't think anyone was looking. It must have been awful hard work keeping the farm going those last few years with both Graden and me gone."

"You sound like you're fixing to blame yourself for that."

"Blame has a way of finding the right place."

"Well, that place ain't with you. Papa lived a hard life long before any of us came along. There's plenty of fifty-three-year old farmers with two healthy sons that never lived to see fifty-four. You gotta stop putting all of this on yourself."

"I should have been with him."

"We still talking about Papa?"

Etta set down her lemonade and reached for my hand.

"Papa's not your fault. Graden's not your fault. It doesn't matter that he was out there to fetch you home. Those men had their eyes set on him, and they would have gotten him anyway, if not that night then on some other."

I stared at the street running past Etta's house, half-expecting to see that dusty white pickup come trundling along with its horrible package in the back. I leaned over and kissed Etta on the forehead, then stood to go back in the house.

"There's plenty of blame for me to take, Etta. There's all of it. Seems like you're the only that don't see it."

◀ ▶

Glenda visited a few weeks before Thanksgiving. I dressed in a heavy brown cotton suit that had been given to me by the teacher in Chicago. It was the only suit I owned, and it fit poorly. I struggled to button my shirt with my crippled right hand.

I didn't know if Glenda would greet me as long-lost family or as an unwelcome presence. She did neither. She was cool, polite, and cautious. She'd grown heavy since I'd last seen her. Her legs and arms were thick, and her hair had turned to grey, but her face was mostly unchanged — her cheeks dark and leathery, her forehead wrinkled at the brow, her eyes set in a squint that made her look perpetually annoyed except on the rare occasions when a broad smile broke out and transformed her entire face.

We hugged each other stiffly inside the doorway and did not touch again before leaving. Our words to each other were guarded. It was that way between Etta and me at first as well, and we had worked through it, but this was different. There was a stillness on both sides, whereas with Etta, the awkwardness had been all mine.

After dinner, Etta's husband and daughter went for a walk, and Etta, Glenda, and I remained at the table. Etta served coffee and peach pie. The conversation started and faded and started and faded again, each change of topic preceded by a weighted hesitation. They spoke mostly of cooking and farming and marriage. Etta tried to draw me in, urging me to tell them where I had been, what my life had been like at school, and what I'd done since then. I began slowly, leaving myself out of the story, talking only of places and dates. I directed my words at the crumbs on the saucer in front of me. Years went by in a matter of a few sentences. Glenda merely nodded. Etta excused herself to clear the dishes, and when she left the table cradling plates and cups, Glenda looked passively through the spoiling chrysanthemums I had brought for the centerpiece and said quietly, "You've been gone a long time."

"Yes."

"You know Mama's in a home?"

"Etta told me, yes."

"She misses him, still."

"I do too."

Glenda scoffed. "That why you ran off and left everything behind?"

"No, I just … couldn't stay there."

"You think you've suffered more than the rest of us."

I couldn't look up at her. I rubbed the remaining fingers on my hand. "I was supposed to take care of him."

Glenda pushed back her chair and collected the remaining plates. I could just hear her over the clatter of utensils.

"Maybe you should have stayed gone."

I didn't reply. She walked into the kitchen, and I stayed at the table alone. After church on Sunday, I said goodbye to Glenda as formally as we had said hello, then returned to my apartment to write a letter to Etta. By Thanksgiving I had moved out of the apartment and was on my way out of Philadelphia.

5

MISSISSIPPI, 1961

MY FATHER WAS THE TOUGHEST man I knew. Graden and I often complained to each other on plucking days and flagged during the brutally hot afternoons, but Papa worked mechanically from dawn until dusk, ignoring blistered palms and the blood seeping from his fingertips. He'd torn toenails and fingernails clean off without so much as pausing, and he'd come into the house some nights with strips of skin hanging like tatters from the bottom of his feet, his flesh so hot that the water-soaked cloths that Mama placed on his forehead were dry within moments, but I couldn't once remember hearing him complain.

He was not a large man, but muscles knotted his arms and legs like twisted tree trunks. He'd often told us that he could strap the rusty plough blade to his back and work just as fast as any mule, and we were never sure whether to believe him or not. He had scars that none of us ever asked him about — raised lines of purplish skin criss-crossing the midnight of his forearms and shoulders. He had dark skin, even by Mississippi standards, and his eyes and teeth were a sickly yellow. When he closed his eyes and mouth, his face was an impenetrable black from which no angles or features could be distinguished. He was kindly to us, but he rarely smiled. We had learned to judge his moods by his hands. They were active when he was angry, either clenched or flexing, and hidden when he was happy, either behind his back or in the folds of his clothes, as if the rare joys he experienced were things that he could grasp and discreetly tuck away.

One day in late September, he did not get out of bed. We all sat at the table spooning a slatelike mix of oatmeal and grits into our mouths while Mama had already set to work behind us, scrubbing away at the pan. Glenda and Etta swung their legs beneath the table, excited because Papa was planning to go to market later that morning to sell the cotton that he had been storing in the shed. Sometimes he would return with a gift for the girls — a hair comb or a bow or once a tin bracelet that they took turns wearing.

"Isn't Papa coming to eat?" Etta asked.

"Never you mind," Mama responded, not bothering to turn around. "You finish up your breakfast and be on about your chores."

They did as they were told, gathering up the clothes bundled on the floor and carrying them out to the tub for washing. Graden and I lingered on, eating more slowly, and questioning each other with glances. Papa was always the first one up in the mornings, and some days when I couldn't sleep, I could hear my father moving around the house before the rooster called out the day. The fact that Mama had not even set out a bowl for him was worrisome. Graden picked up his own bowl, with a few meagre spoonfuls left in it. He headed towards our parents' bedroom, and I quickly rose to follow.

It was the first time we had seen our father sick. He had thrown off the bed sheets and he lay there, sweating profusely and staring at the ceiling. He turned his head to look at us in the doorway, but his eyes were unfocussed. His breathing was gravelly and weak and a trail of spit glistened across his cheek.

Mama was right behind us and slapped at the backs of our heads, screaming for us to get out. She was fiercely protective of Papa, and I suppose she didn't want us to see him in a weakened state. Graden dropped his bowl and it clanged off the floor and rolled as the two of us hurried out of the house.

We went straight to work. We walked through the rows in unusual silence, picking handfuls of dew-heavy cotton and keeping mostly to ourselves. When we broke at midday, we returned to the house. We ate potatoes and thin strips of fish while Mama glared at us. When we were finished, she nodded at me.

"Your father's been asking for you."

I went back to the bedroom, but would not advance past the doorway. The room smelled of filth. Papa was sitting upright in the bed, swaying slightly, his skin a palish grey. When he spoke, he used as few words as possible.

"How many sacks?"

I tried to picture the sacks of cotton already sitting in the shed, plus the few we had been able to gather that morning, but I didn't know how many.

Before I could answer, Graden appeared at my shoulder.

"Fourteen, sir."

I kicked Graden's ankle sharply in the hope he would leave, but he barely flinched.

Papa continued, "You know the way to town?"

"Yes, sir," Graden and I answered in unison. I jabbed Graden with a quick elbow, then added, "I can drive the truck, sir."

In truth, I had never taken the truck off the farm and had only driven it a few times at that, but it was still something that I could do that Graden couldn't. His interruption irked me. Papa asked for *me*, not Graden. I wanted to show Papa that I could handle the responsibility, and maybe I wanted to prove that to Graden as well. Papa lay back down and pulled the sheet around him. It was settled.

Graden would not be talked out of going to town under any circumstances. We argued the whole time that we loaded the bed of the truck with the sacks of cotton, and in the end I relented. I could not go alone, and Graden, despite being only fifteen, had already grown to be strong and tall enough that he would give pause to anyone thinking of starting trouble.

Our truck was a 1941 Ford that had been all but left for dead by a grocery store owner in town. During the winter months Papa took on whatever odd jobs he could find, and after repairing the roof of the grocery, he negotiated for the truck in lieu of payment. Papa had driven it, rattling and sputtering, up to the house with a grin on his face like he'd found gold. He spent the next few weeks cleaning and tuning it, and it had served us well since, although it could be fussy at times.

The engine turned over easily, but I stalled it twice just backing away from the shed and easing it out past the front yard. Graden had the good sense not to say anything, but I knew he was watching closely and thinking that he could do better. The truck bounced and lurched along the rutted track. It rolled along more smoothly once I made it to the road, but I kept my grip tight on the wheel, regardless. Graden sat beside me on the bench seat, his head bobbing with each jolt from ridges in the hardpan of dried clay. I was focussed on the road, but I checked over my shoulder often, making sure that the sacks were still securely in place.

The engine whined and occasionally coughed smoke that wafted up from the front grill. I'd told Papa I could drive the truck, but I realized that I had no idea how to fix it if it broke down, which he said it was sometimes wont to do. I wondered what would happen if we found ourselves stranded on the side of the road, but I knew Graden was watching and so I tried not to look concerned.

We'd both been to town before, but never without Mama or Papa. I'd helped my father unload last year's cotton and had met the merchant, Mr. Stevenson, but I'd waited outside the store while the men went inside to complete the sale.

"I can take the wheel for a spell."

I glanced at Graden. I was sweating and my arms were sore, but I didn't want to look weak in front of my younger brother.

"Papa told *me* to take the truck."

"Papa's not here. I was just offering to help."

"Don't need your help," I said. Then embarrassed by the harshness of my tone, I added, "We ain't got much longer. Town is just up ahead."

In truth, I was not sure how much farther it was, but the patches of trees along the side of the road had started to thin, and we'd already passed a few isolated houses carved out from the land, so I felt sure we were getting close. I'd thought the road might get smoother as we got closer to town, but in fact it got worse. The heavier traffic caused deep furrows on wet days, which then dried into a criss-crossed series of ridges that I had to navigate carefully to avoid getting stuck.

I had never driven in traffic, and I panicked when the first car came rolling slowly towards us, also carefully picking its way along the road. I turned out of its way too sharply, taking the right front wheel off the road, then had to fight to keep the truck from rolling into the ditch.

I fared better as we got into town. There were more cars, but the roads were wider and paved as well, and I was growing more comfortable. I kept my eyes straight ahead, but Graden took in everything, turning this way and that to examine the buildings and the stalls and the solitary gas pump on the main corner. He met the eyes of all who looked at him, whether they were white or black.

Mr. Stevenson's store was a third of the way down a long side street, tucked between a hardware store and a laundry. I took the truck to the end of the street, then circled around so I could park around the back, as I had seen our father do. Mr. Stevenson was a thin man with a slight stoop, who tried to cover his balding head with a few long strands of black and grey hair that he combed over from the side. He stood in the doorway at the back of the store and watched us get out of the truck.

"You're James Williams's boy."

"Yes, sir. I was here last year, sir."

"I remember. Where's your pa?"

"He's sick, sir. He sent me." I waved to indicate Graden. "Us. This is my brother, Graden."

Mr. Stevenson ignored the introduction. He stepped out from the doorway to look at the sacks of cotton on the back of the truck. He grunted and spat.

"You can park by that post over there. Bring your goods into the stockroom here when you're done."

I thanked him and moved the truck as he directed. Mr. Stevenson stood by as we unloaded the sacks. Inside, a pungent smell of live-stock assaulted our nostrils. His backroom was dark except for a few slats of sunshine slipping in through gaps in the walls, and the air was thick with dust. By the time we had finished unloading the truck, the legs of our coveralls were coated with thin white fibres and our ankles itched ceaselessly where they had gotten on our skin.

When we were done, Mr. Stevenson waved us outside while he went in to examine the cotton.

"We supposed to just wait here?" asked Graden.

"Shhh."

"What if he doesn't give us anything?"

"Be quiet! I been here before, not you. Just be still. Don't cause no trouble."

We could hear the old man shuffling around in the darkened room, could see him moving in and out of the dusty shafts of light. He called his son in from the front of the store, and one by one they hauled the sacks on to a scale. He opened each bag and ran his hand through the white fibres, assessing them. He came back out with a smile on his face.

"Well, I must say, your old man does know how to run a field. Them bags is pretty even for measure. I can give you a dollar and eighty-five cents on the bag. That's an even twenty dollars for the lot."

Mr. Stevenson reached into his pocket and started counting out one-dollar bills. Graden shuffled his feet, but looked steadily at him.

"We brung fourteen sacks, sir."

I stiffened and watched my brother from the corner of my eye. Mr. Stevenson stopped counting and looked up at Graden.

"Yup. I counted 'em, boy. Don't you worry."

"But that ain't right, sir. A dollar eight-five a sack is twenty-five dollars and ninety cents."

Mr. Stevenson's expression darkened, but Graden either took no notice or ignored the warning.

"You saying I'm cheating you?"

"No, sir. Maybe you made a mistake, sir. I can show you."

I stepped in front of Graden. "Please don't pay him no mind, sir."

"Don't pay him no mind? Well, that's an odd request considering he just called me either a cheat or an idiot. Now listen here. I done right by your old man. I dealt with him for a lot of years, and I always been fair, but don't think that I need some nigger boy coming to my store to insult me!"

Graden didn't respond, but he didn't step back or look away, either. I turned to him, pleading, "Just get back in the truck. This ain't the time for you to be fancy."

Graden did as he was asked, and I turned back to Mr. Stevenson, whose gaunt face was now flushed with rage.

"You know I'm the only man in town that will buy cotton from a nigger? I imagine your father is going to tan your hide something awful when you go back to him with a truck full of cotton and no money."

He turned as if to walk back into the store, then stopped and seemed to collect himself.

"I'll tell you what I will do, boy. I will give you thirteen dollars, and you can be on your way. I only do this for your father's sake."

I had no means with which to argue. I accepted the thirteen dollars and thanked him and apologized again for my brother. When I opened the truck door, Graden was shouting before I could climb up into the cab.

"He cheated us!"

"I know that," I yelled back, although in truth I'd had no idea until Graden had spoken up.

"Well, what are we going to do?"

"Nothing. That's what. You done opened your mouth, and now we got thirteen dollars instead of twenty. You want to go back out there and talk some more? Maybe we'll get nothing instead of thirteen, and maybe you'll get a beating out of it too. And maybe I'll let him do it!"

Graden leaned back and looked away.

"That ain't right."

"Right's got nothing to do with it," I said.

"Right's got everything to do with it."

I told him to shut up and for once he listened. I was angry at Graden, but it wasn't only because of the money, and the trouble he had almost started. I was also angry because he had expected me to deal with the situation, and I didn't know how to. I was flustered and kept flooding the engine. It took me three tries to get the truck started. The ride home felt longer than the ride into town, but it was just as silent.

6

AMBLAN, 2008

I THUMBED THE WHEEL on the binoculars and brought the black-rimmed world into focus. The bread stacked in rows in the window of the store down the street. The salt pellets sinking slowly through the ice on the sidewalk. The old man sorting through money in the back of the cab.

The man extended one shaking hand across the seat, the cabbie reaching over his shoulder to take the fare. The door opened on the side facing me. I adjusted the binoculars again, watching the man rest both feet on the ground, then grab the top of the door with one hand and half-push, half-pull himself to a not-quite-upright position. I studied his face. Weathered, sagging. Tired. I tried to subtract each line in my mind, each crease, raising the cheeks, brightening the eyes, trying to match the face to one I last saw forty-three years ago.

I thought I would know when I saw him — just know — but I didn't. I couldn't be sure, but I had to be.

The man tapped the back of the cab as it pulled away. He wore a thin Kangol-style cap, and the collar of his coat was open. He looked accustomed to the cold. He stepped on to the sidewalk, shuffling along slowly to the store entrance and went inside.

I folded the binoculars and put them back in the case on the seat beside me, then picked up my camera and snapped a few quick photos. The engine of the rented Ford Explorer was off. I watched the door of the shop for a moment, then turned the ignition, and drove off.

◀ ▶

I tucked a newspaper under my arm and entered the coffee shop, shaking the snow from my jacket and hanging it over the coat rack. It fell from its hook, and I bent over to pick it up, my knee groaning its displeasure at the unwanted strain. I hung the garment back on the rack, more securely this time, then draped my hat and scarf across it.

As I crossed the floor and selected a table that was free in the corner, I could feel the watchful eye of the manager. He was leaning against the serving window between the kitchen and the counter. I seated myself and gave him a brief nod. He returned it and offered a curt smile, then half-turned towards the kitchen, reading order tags hung from the spin tray like some ragtag Christmas tree. It was a reaction I'd seen many times before. I guessed that they probably didn't see many black folks in these parts. Or maybe just not many strangers.

A waitress flipped over the empty cup in front of me, filled it, and offered me a menu.

"Thank you, ma'am. Just the coffee's fine."

I produced a handful of change from my pocket and started fingering through the coins, separating the Canadian from the American, until I had matched the total. I watched her walk away. The shop was about a third full, and she stopped at several other tables on her way back to the register. I spread the newspaper out in front of me, pulled a pair of reading glasses from my shirt pocket, and sipped on my coffee.

"What happened to your hand, mister?"

I looked up and looked over the rim of my glasses. A young boy, maybe five or six, stood by the table, strands of brown hair hanging limply from under his toque, like the woolen mittens dangling on yarn from the sleeves of his coat.

"Thomas!"

His mother shot towards him, a short, doughy-faced woman whose cheeks flushed in reaction to her son's question. I tried to be subtle as I pulled my hand away from the edge of the newspaper and out of sight under the table.

"I'm so sorry."

"Not a problem, ma'am."

"Thomas, you know better than to be rude to people. Apologize to the gentleman."

"Sorry, sir."

I muttered another "no problem" and waited for them to leave. The mother turned to me instead.

"My son's curiosity sometimes gets the best of his manners. You know how it is with young boys."

I nodded.

"I don't believe we've seen you around before. Are you new to Amblan?"

"Just visiting, ma'am."

She held her hand to her chest and smiled broadly.

"Why, I just love your accent. I'm good with accents. Let me guess: Kentucky?"

I set the paper down and sat upright in the booth, then removed my glasses, and set them on the table. The manager was still looking at orders on the rack, but I could tell he was no longer paying attention to them.

"Mississippi."

"I knew it! I knew I was close. Well, I'm Margaret, and this here is my boy, Thomas. Welcome to our little town."

"Nice to meet you. Thanks."

She waited for my name, but I didn't offer it. After a second or two, she continued, "I imagine all this snow and cold must be quite a change for you, coming from Mississippi and all."

"I've spent a fair bit of time in the northern states. I'll survive."

She leaned forward slightly, as if to share a secret, and I stiffened reflexively, keeping one eye on the manager. Margaret was puzzled for a moment, but continued, "Well, the northern states ain't the same as northern Ontario. Things are pretty tepid right now, but there's a right storm coming this way. I suggest you keep yourself someplace cozy, 'cause when they hit, they hit in a hurry. No time to be out on the roads, if it ain't something you're used to."

The boy was starting to fidget beside her, as anxious to leave as I was to see them go. I looked at the manager, who had now moved closer, under the pretense of wiping the counter. I spoke lower.

"Some of them roads up in the hills, I imagine they must get tricky."

"Humph! When things turn bad like they're supposed to soon, those roads up in the hills get damn near impassable."

Thomas looked up at her, and she blushed.

"Darn near impassable, I guess I should say."

I sipped my coffee, then reached for my reading glasses, and put them back on.

"Well ... I sure appreciate the warning."

Margaret beamed at me. "You have a good day, sir."

She prodded Thomas in the back, and they walked on. I didn't turn, but I watched them leave in the mirror that was hanging above the service window. Behind them, a taxi wobbled past, drunken and distorted in the mirror's reflection. I took another sip from my coffee and returned to my paper. I kept my hand under the table.

7

MISSISSIPPI, 1961

WE KEPT THE SECRET from our father for six days. He remained in bed for three days after our trip to town. On the fourth day we heard him scuttling about the kitchen in the dust-coloured dawn and just as quickly heard Mama's animated whispers, telling him to get back to bed for more rest. On the fifth day he woke vigorously and ordered Mama to fix him up a colossal breakfast — six eggs with two thick slices of crusty bread and a half-inch thick slab of ham — but he ate little, his appetite fading after a few triumphant mouthfuls. He went out to the porch to sit in the weak sunlight and, after a reluctant nod of the head from Mama, Graden and I pounced on his plate, slathering our fingers and chins with grease, while Etta and Glenda watched with reservation. After a short time on the porch, Papa sank back into his previous state and spent the rest of the day in bed.

We woke on the sixth day to the sound of wood splitting in the backyard. We found our father, axe in hand, sweating and still gaunt, but no longer as hollowed out as he had been the previous days. We stacked wood as he split and knew by the pace that his strength had returned.

We worked through the morning without saying a word. Mama poked her head out the back door and called us for lunch. I had spent the hours outside racking my brain for a way to avoid telling my father the truth, and in the end I'd decided the simplest thing was to say that Mr. Stevenson had short-changed us. It would be believable enough — the reason Papa always went to town himself was to prevent us from being taken advantage of — and it would make sense that, feeling ashamed of the fact, I would wait as long as possible to tell him what had happened. I dipped my hands into the water bucket and started rubbing them clean, turning myself so that I would not have to look at my father when I told the story, but Graden spoke first.

"I think Mr. Stevenson's been cheating you, sir."

I turned in shock, eyes wide. Papa looked at Graden as well, but his face was calm. He said nothing.

"His figures didn't add up. We brung fourteen sacks, but he wasn't going to pay for fourteen sacks. Warren and I tried to explain it to him, but he just got real angry."

I flinched at hearing my name. Graden's expression was unchanged, and I realized that he actually thought he was helping. That he was giving me credit for standing up alongside him, when it wasn't true. I wanted no part of it then, and I wanted no part of it now. I shrunk against the side of the house as I dried my hands on an old rag and waited for my father's anger.

It didn't come. Papa stared at Graden for a few moments, then spoke quietly.

"Go on in the house."

He walked away from us. We did as we were told, but he didn't join us. He picked up his axe again, and we ate corn and strips of ham leftover from breakfast in the kitchen, listening to the rhythm of his chopping.

◄ ►

I was getting ready for bed when Mama appeared in the doorway.

"Your father wants to talk to you. He's on the porch."

Papa was holding a thin, hand-rolled cigarette and blowing wisps of smoke into the dark blue dusk. He had built a bench, and he gestured for me to sit beside him.

"I bought this from a Mr. Parson."

For a moment, I thought he was referring to the cigarette, but Papa was gazing out over the yard, at the carefully groomed dirt lawn and the chestnut tree.

"There wasn't no house on it then. It was just a scrubby patch of trees and bushes. Been cleared once, of the big trees, but then had overgrown again. Your uncle and I spent the better part of a year re-clearing it. Cut down all those trees and bushes, pulled out all those stumps. Hauled one rock out of the ground the size of a pig. Some of that wood I sold. Some of it I used to build this house. Most of it, well, Mr. Parson sent a few boys over and they just took it. Wasn't much I could do about it."

I sat silently, studying my father. There was a lantern on the porch, but my father never liked to light it because of the insects. My father was just a shape in the darkness, a shadow shrouded in sweet-smelling smoke.

"Your brother's a smart one. And brave too, ain't no arguing against that. But every man has his place in the world, and there ain't much mercy for a man who tries to change that. I hear these men on the radio sometimes, talking about changing things, talking about protestin' and the like. But those men ain't from here. Some of 'em might be from Mississippi, but they ain't from *this* Mississippi."

Papa raised the cigarette to his lips, and the faint glow seemed to shine off the lighter-coloured scar tissue criss-crossing his forearm. I had never been curious about the scars before, but now I couldn't stop looking at them.

"I heard Mr. Parson sold that wood for a good penny. Stuffed his pockets real good off this property, too. I knew I was paying more than what someone else would have had to, but that's the way it is. I could have fought, but then what would I have now? Sometimes a little common sense beats a whole lot of courage."

Papa turned and leaned in towards me, close enough that I could make out his face. His eyes were yellow, and I realized that he was drunk.

"I ain't as dumb as your brother thinks I am. And he ain't as smart as he thinks he is. All them figures and science and history he learns, those are things that I ain't ever gonna know, but I know things that he ain't ever gonna learn, either. I know how to survive. Graden don't. All those smarts ain't gonna do nothing but get him in trouble. You need to look out for him. You hear me?"

"Yes, sir."

Papa turned his gaze back towards the darkness, and when no more was said, I got up to leave. Graden was lying in bed. The lantern was lit, and he was writing figures on a sheet of paper. I watched him for a moment, replaying my father's words in my head, until the meaning of them finally was clear. Papa was afraid of Graden. Not afraid for him, but of him. And I realized that I was a little afraid of him too. Papa had called him "brave," but that was the wrong word. Graden was fearless, and that fearlessness made him dangerous, to himself and to all of us. Graden was capable of anything, and that realization terrified me, but also excited me.

I sat beside him on the bed and looked at the sheet of numbers. Some of it looked familiar from the few classes that I'd taken, but most of it was not.

"Can you show me that?"

Graden held the sheet towards me so I could see it.

"No, I mean *show* me that. How to do that."

Graden hesitated, thinking it was some joke. Then he smiled broadly and handed me an empty sheet of paper and a spare pencil. We stayed up until early morning.

8

AMBLAN, 2008

I LEFT ONE COPY of a photo of the man in the taxi in an envelope in the foyer message slot, with instructions for faxing, and then went up to the room. There were no hotels in town, but Etta had made some phone calls and found someone with a room for rent. The room was one of three on the second storey of an aging country-style home, which had been shoddily partitioned to house tenants. My door opened on to a square living space, just large enough to hold a small desk. To the right, a cramped and mouldy bathroom, and straight ahead, the bedroom. There was no furniture save the bed — a musty mattress laid flat on springs — that rolled across the floor if I moved in my sleep and a lamp, placed directly on the floor. The floor was cracked and faded hardwood, and when I removed my shoes, I could feel the cold through my socks.

I laid my hat, gloves, and scarf on the desk, but chose to keep my coat on. I carried my small bag into the bedroom, opened it, and laid the other copy of the photo on the bed. The lamp's light was barely strong enough to reach beyond its shade. I opened the curtains and felt a blast of cold against my thigh. The wind whistled through a small crack at the bottom corner of the window, the line of it traced with frost. Beyond the window, a diner backed onto an alley where black garbage bags had been pecked open by blacker crows that were hopping about the strewn trash and caw-ing a raucous symphony to their found treasure.

I walked around to the other side of the bed to keep from blocking the light and examined the picture again. Eight men walking down the front steps of a Mississippi courthouse. I re-membered standing there, most of the men wearing pressed suits and freshly shined shoes, smiling and shaking hands, all charges against them having been thrown out. The men who killed my brother.

On one side of the steps, a crowd of whites were cheering, clapping, and whistling; greeting them like heroes. Someone reached out to pass them cigars. On the other side of the steps, I was gathered among a group of black men and women, young, angry, and impotent. No signs or slogans or even shouts, for fear of retribution. A hard-eyed white man who reeked of Klan watched us from the other side, scanning our faces, writing down names. One white man holding about sixty blacks silent, with nothing but a pad and a pen.

I tried to match the face in the photo on the bed to the face of one of the men walking down those steps, the freshly shaven young man in simple pants and a plain white shirt, standing be-side his father.

I wavered. I looked at the photo of the man and at the other photos and files that I'd laid out. There were police records, FBI interviews, testimonies that had taken decades to extract be-cause of fear, and one autopsy report. The cold, clinical summa-tion of the life of Graden Williams.

I flipped through the pages of the autopsy report, as I had countless times before. There was no anger anymore; just a cold feeling. I preferred the anger, and each time I opened the report, I wished that I could muster it again.

I let the autopsy report drop to the bed, the black-and-white photo of my brother's body falling beside the picture of the old man on the street. There were dark blotches across Graden's body. Some were severe burns, others were places where the moss had eaten through the skin. His lower jaw was blue and swollen and set at an angle that did not match the upper. There were other cuts and bruises, and his right arm was bent in too many places. He had been castrated, and they had stuffed the testicles into his mouth.

The coroner had ruled the cause of death to be drowning. They had found enough water in his lungs to know that he was still breathing when they had dumped him in the swamp. It was the only photo I had of my brother.

I pulled my coat tight around my neck and stared out the window at nothing. In the alley below I could still hear the chorus of crows as they picked contentedly amongst the scraps.

9

MISSISSIPPI, 1963

THE FROSTS THAT YEAR held until the first week of November. We spent a couple of weeks cleaning the field, then settled in for the slow period that would stretch until mid-to-late February, when it would come time to start prepping the ground for spring planting. There was still work to do — minor repairs on the house, chopping and stacking piles of wood, clearing out another portion of land for future planting — but we had much more idle time during the winter months and that meant more time for lessons.

After that first night, listening to Papa's warning on the front porch then seeing Graden hunched over his papers and finally asking him to teach me, I spent every evening studying with Graden by lantern or by candlelight. I was slow to learn at first and frustrated. Graden seemed to pick things up so easily while I had to ask to have the same thing shown to me again and again, but Graden was patient with me and after several months, I had advanced to the point where I could understand most of the lessons he taught me the first time through. I caught Graden once, incorrectly summing a series of numbers, and although I tried to hide my pride and excitement I could not sleep the rest of the night.

Even though Papa needed his help, Graden still managed to slip away to school most days, and eventually our father stopped trying to hold him back. I used to resent the days that Graden snuck out of chores, but now I felt something else. Jealousy. It was compounded by the fact that Papa spent those days in a sour mood, working me extra hard as if he held me somehow responsible.

The only consolation was that I knew that whatever Graden learned on those days, he would share with me at night. I would hold my pencil in fingers sliced raw and swollen from picking cotton, leaning in close to make out the words and numbers in the flickering light. Graden would sit across from me, fiddling with paper and pencil, pretending to work on a lesson, but most times he was already done and just waiting for me to finish.

Graden had continued to grow tall and strong. At seventeen, he was a head taller than I was and outweighed me by a good fifteen to twenty pounds. I continued to pull bullying pranks on him to try to maintain my superiority, but in the end I realized that he tolerated them not out of meekness, but with a weary patience, and I wondered if this had always been so.

One night, late in November, I heard shuffling in the darkness in the bedroom.

"You getting the lantern?"

"Not tonight. We'll do double lessons tomorrow."

I sat up in bed. My brother was dressing hastily in the moonlight.

"What are you doing?"

"I can't tell you. Go back to bed. Don't say nothing."

Graden knew exactly which floorboards in the house would squeak and which wouldn't. He moved silently into the hallway and was gone. It seemed like a long time that he was gone, but it was difficult for me to tell. It may have only been a couple of hours. When Graden returned, he removed his clothes and slid back into bed without a word.

◄ ►

Graden's secrecy bothered me more than I wanted to admit. He was sneaking out at night once a week, never saying where he was going. Around that same time, I started to slip away some evenings as well, cutting through the woods and up the road to a hillside shack where a few other boys from neighbouring farms would gather. We'd tune the radio to whatever music we could find through the static — Duke Ellington, Sam Cooke, Buddy Holly. We'd play cards and pass around cheap cigarettes and drink foul-tasting gin or moonshine. Mississippi was a dry state in name only, and booze was never hard to come by. If cotton indeed were king, then alcohol was surely a prince.

A few of the more liberal-minded girls would show up now and then, and the group of us would dance late into the night before some coupled to go a little farther up the hill to find a private spot while the others drifted home. The shack was set far enough back from the road to avoid attention, and cars rarely passed through that area at night anyway, but we were still cautious not to let things get too loud.

On these nights, I would tiptoe back into the house with great exaggeration and wait for Graden to ask where I'd been so that I could spitefully tell him it was none of his business. But Graden never asked. He could certainly smell the gin and the smoke on my clothing, and after I had lagged through the day, I felt sure that Papa knew about it as well, but nothing was said.

On the nights when we were both home, we continued to light the kerosene lamp and work through the math problems, history questions, or readings that Graden had been assigned, but more and more often we worked in silence.

One day, I pulled Glenda and Etta aside and asked them if they knew where Graden went at night — I wondered if he had said anything to them — but they were puzzled. They hadn't known he was sneaking out at all.

My brother left the house on the same night every week: on

Tuesday. Finally, I couldn't stand it any longer. I had to find out where he was going. One night, I turned the lamp off at bedtime and slipped under the covers with my clothes still on. I waited for Graden to get up and leave, then counted to thirty and rose to follow him.

I went out the back door and looked around. The nights in winter were eerily quiet. No chirping crickets or bellowing bullfrogs. I spotted Graden halfway through the cotton field and waited for him to finish crossing before following him. Strands of spider webs caressed my shins and ankles, and I could feel my pants getting damp from the moisture that was beginning to collect already on the few remaining leaves. The moon was mostly hidden by clouds, and as intimately as I knew the field, I still had to move carefully on the uneven ground.

On my own nights out I'd turn left after the field, cut through the woods, and loop back on to the road to the gin shack. Graden turned right. He continued along the edge of the property, marked by a shallow ravine that had once been a creek, but had dried up long ago. He picked up a long, thin branch and inched his way over the edge. I counted off the seconds again in my head. When I reached the edge, Graden was still there, just below the lip. He held a lantern that he'd just lighted.

"If you're coming, you should get yourself a stick."

"For what?"

Graden inclined his head towards the wild grass and bulrushes lining what would have been the creek bed. "Snakes."

"Where the hell you going? Ain't nothing out this way but the Townsend and the Dale farms."

Graden shrugged and walked away, swishing the stick through the grass in front of him to ward off any snakes. I looked around for a stick of my own.

◀ ▶

The Townsends were sharecroppers. They lived and worked on a farm, but they didn't own it. They'd moved onto the land a few years back, and Mama and the girls had gone over to welcome them with a pie, but we had seen and talked to them very little since. When Graden and I reached their backyard, I was surprised to see lights on in the barn. As we climbed up the short bank, I could hear voices. For the thirty minutes or so that we had walked along the creek, Graden had said nothing to me about where we were headed.

A person stood outside the barn door and raised a lantern.

"It's me. Graden Williams."

"Who you got with you?"

"This is my brother, Warren."

The face peered around the edge of the upraised lantern.

"All right, then. The more the better, I guess."

The man opened the barn door, and Graden dropped his stick in the yard and shook the man's hand.

There were close to forty people inside. I recognized most, but not all, of them. Lanterns hung from the beams, glowing balls surrounded by swarms of insects. The floor had been swept clean and bales of hay had been neatly stacked along the sides of the barn. Chaff from the bales drifted idly, coming to rest in the hair and clothes of the people gathered, or touching the lamps and instantly singing out of existence.

Everyone was packed tightly together and dressed in dark clothes so that they could arrive and leave, hidden by night. Those closest to the door greeted Graden warmly but quietly, and I trailed along in his wake. There were a few women, but mostly the crowd was made up of men. Their faces were serious and their eyes scanned back and forth constantly, even though the barn had no windows.

"What is this?" I whispered to Graden.

"This is where I've been coming. Every Tuesday."

"For what?"

"You'll see."

At the far end of the barn, Mr. Townsend was talking with a light-skinned man I'd never seen before. He was dressed like a farmer, in coveralls and a white shirt, but his clothes gave him away nonetheless. His shirt was too clean — no yellowing or discolouration from sweat — and the hems of his coveralls were neat, not frayed. Mr. Townsend was taller than him, but Mr. Townsend slouched and bowed his head so he was still looking up to this young stranger, who stood straight and confident. The man turned to inspect the crowd and nodded to two similarly dressed young men on his right.

"OK, let's get started."

The three gathered together, but all attention was focussed on the man who had been conversing with Mr. Townsend. If I strained to listen, I could hear a clear northern accent. I'd heard voices like it on the radio from time to time, but I'd never actually seen a northerner before, and I stiffened, recalling my father's warning about looking after Graden.

At the front of the barn, the stranger smiled widely and clasped his hands together.

"It's almost time. I know you've all been doing a lot of meeting and planning, and I assure you, you are not alone. The same meetings and the same plans have been taking place throughout this county and in counties across Mississippi, because, brothers and sisters, we are all united by one desire — dignity."

There was a murmuring of approval in the crowd, but there was a palpable sense of uneasiness as well.

"The government of the United States says that we are equal to any white man in this country, even the president himself. In fact, we have the power to pick the president. We have that choice. We have that *right*. But there are those who don't want to see us exercise it. There are those who still think that they should make all our decisions for us."

The murmuring became louder and more certain. I placed my hand on Graden's elbow and whispered, "We shouldn't be here. This is trouble."

"This isn't trouble," he replied. "Trouble is that gin shack you spend so many nights at. This is progress. This is a chance to *change* things."

"This is a chance to get killed, that's what this is! Papa will whip us both if he finds out."

"I know he will. But that's because this is something that Papa can't ever understand."

Graden turned his attention back to the young man standing in front of us. He was talking now about buses going to Jackson, and voter registrations and rallies. I could see beads of sweat on his forehead, and the people closest to him were swaying, as if they were listening to hymns. So this was where Graden had been coming for the last two or three months.

I remember thinking that Graden was wrong, and that Papa understood this kind of thing all too well. Papa would know that a meeting like this was trouble, that these young, light-skinned men at the front of the barn were exactly the kind of people he was talking about when he said they didn't know *this* Mississippi.

Here was my chance to tell Graden about my conversation with Papa, about how dangerous this all was, and about how courage was not always the best course, but I looked at the rapt expression on Graden's face and knew he would not be dissuaded. And I knew that wherever this led, I would go with him.

◀ ▶

On New Year's Eve it snowed. We'd seen snow before of course, but never like this. It came so thick it seemed to be falling in layers, like something had ruptured in the sky and was spilling out across every house and farm and road, turning the world white for as far as we could see. It carried on through the night and by morning there was snow on the ground halfway up our shins. We didn't own boots, but on the first day of 1964 we ran out of the house anyway, sinking into it, falling, rolling, rising, and throwing ourselves into it again.

Etta came out in just a dress, and Mama yelled at her from the porch not to get it wet, but Etta didn't listen and Mama, seeing her skipping and leaping around the yard, didn't repeat the warning. Glenda took the time to change into warmer clothes, then wandered slowly with her hands outstretched, palms turned upwards, catching slowly falling flakes then letting them melt between her fingers.

I sat down in a small drift that had collected beside the porch and lifted a handful of snow into my mouth. Etta continued to dance through the snow and Glenda began to sing. I felt a sudden spear of ice along my spine and gasped in shock. I turned to see Graden laughing, his hands white with evidence of the snow that he had dropped down the back of my shirt. My skin burned with cold, and my breath shuddered out from my mouth in bursts of grey.

"You're dead!" I shouted.

I crawled towards him on all fours and grabbed him by the leg. I tackled him and pushed his face into the ground, but he continued to laugh anyway, and I could not help doing the same. The girls joined in as well, pointing at us and giggling as we wrestled beneath the tree, soaked through and shivering, but delirious. Etta took Glenda's hand and Papa stepped out onto the porch to put his arm around Mama's waist, and I held Graden's face down with my forearm, knowing all the while that he could throw me off with a shrug anytime he chose. I wished that it would snow every day.

10

AMBLAN, 2008

MY EXPERIENCE CONSISTED of three women. The first was a white girl at a roadside shack back in Mississippi. She was drunk and had dragged her friend out to the black section of the county on a dare. We danced, nothing more, but still she'd nearly cost me my hand.

The second was an arts student at Loyola University, the first person I'd known other than Graden who believed the world could be changed by ideas. I had learned early that the world is defined by what you do, not by what you think, but she was full of the kind of optimism that can only be held by those who have been sheltered from reality. And yet her passion for everything she did won me over for a short time. Our relationship was mostly platonic as well. There were a few occasions of intimacy, but they were clumsy and unnatural. She could give in to the moment completely, but I could not.

The third was a whore I took in Minnesota. My co-workers had urged me on and had even taken up a collection. My actions were timid and uncertain. She guided me through my part patiently, but when I tried to convince her to stay and talk afterwards, she collected the money, kissed me on the cheek, and walked out without a word. I said nothing about it to the others. When they asked me about how it was, I looked down at the tops of my shoes, and they didn't press me.

◄ ►

Looking out the window of the rented room, I could see a woman standing on the front doorstep. I hoped she would go away, but she pressed the buzzer again, and I turned to shuffle down the stairway. When I opened the door, I could see that she was older than she had appeared to be from upstairs. She might have been in her mid-forties, but her skin was still smooth except for a few wrinkles around her eyes. She wore a heavy coat, but had the hood thrown back despite the cold, and wisps of brown hair twisted about her ears in the wind.

"I saw you on the news," she said.

I blinked and loosened my grip on the doorknob.

"I see." I hesitated. "OK."

I stepped aside, and she followed me. The front door of the house opened on to a small living room that had been clumsily converted into a reception area for tenants. It held little more than three mismatched couches crowded together and angled around a faux-antique coffee table. The woman removed her boots and tossed her coat and scarf across the back of one of the couches before sitting down. I admired the line of her jaw, the smoothness of her neck, her pearl-coloured collarbone, but I wasn't drawn to her. I had come to hate beauty. She declined my offer of coffee or tea, and so I sat across from her on the opposite couch.

"I guess you must be the one who called."

"Yes. I'm Miriam." She leaned forward to shake my hand, but I just nodded. She sat back and looked around the room, then back at me.

"I'm sorry about your brother."

"Long time ago."

"Still a terrible thing. And still hurts, I'm sure. I'm guessing you wouldn't be here otherwise. I lost a husband. It was years ago. Heart attack. I guess it's not really the same ..." Her words trailed off. She cleared her throat and tried to compose herself. "Maybe I will have a cup of coffee after all," she said.

I rose and went into the kitchen to put on a pot. I could see the edge of her around the corner.

"I was at my cousin's place in Windsor when I saw the news piece. When they put that picture up of the eight of them, I was sure as anything that it was Earl. Later on, when they said that fella in the photo was dead, I wasn't so sure. I mean, it's hard to look at someone and imagine that they could do something like that. It's just something you can't believe. I couldn't get that feeling out of my head, though. Took me a few days before I decided to call."

Returning with two cups of coffee, I placed one in front of her and sat on the opposite couch.

"Earl Daniel?"

"Yes. At least I guess so. That's how we all know him here."

"How long's he been here?"

"I can't say. I've only been here six years myself, so he's been here at least that long."

"Do you know him well?"

"No. I mean, it's a small place, so everyone knows everyone some. I haven't spoken to him much. He keeps mostly to himself. Seems to be well liked, though."

Her voice tailed off at the end, as if she had just remembered who she was speaking to.

"I guess that don't hold much water with you, though."

We sipped our coffees and spoke for a half an hour, with her doing most of the talking. I questioned her about the man's habits, his health, who he knew, what visitors he had, and how often. She told me a little about her life, although I told her nothing about at all about my own. She explained that she had moved up here to be with her husband, whom she'd met on camping trip. It was her second marriage. The first husband had left her after ten years. The second husband died young, and suddenly. I asked why she had stayed here after his death, and she didn't have an answer, but she told me about the tightness and warmth of the community.

"Can I ask you ... what's it like? Chasing something like this your whole life? I mean, I admire it, but do you ever think that maybe your brother would just want you to move on? Do something else?"

"Maybe he would. But I was never very good at doing what my brother wanted."

She nodded, rather than prodding further, and I was grateful to her for it.

"So what happens next?" she asked. "Will the police be involved?"

"Not yet. No sense getting everyone riled up until I'm sure. Does anyone else know you called?"

"My cousin, yes. But no one from around here. I felt silly even thinking it, to be honest with you, but I just couldn't shake that picture. Just struck me somehow, you know? Like instinct or something."

I collected the empty cups and took them into the kitchen. She took the hint and rose from the couch.

"What if it's him? TV said that everyone else is either dead or in jail, right? So this would be the end of it. What would you do?"

"I don't know," I said, returning from the kitchen. "It doesn't matter. I spent most of my life doing nothing. Doing nothing is always easy to go back to. For now I just ... just need to know."

I caught the scent of her perfume as I handed her coat to her and she wrapped a scarf around her neck, She paused in the doorway.

"You seem like a nice man, Mr. Williams. For what it's worth, I hope it's not him. I just wouldn't want something like that to be true."

11

MISSISSIPPI, 1964

THE SUMMER BEFORE GRADEN DIED, I sat beside him on a crowded school bus on its way to Jackson. There had been two more meetings since the one that I had attended, but the well-dressed young men from the north were absent. Graden explained that they had come from all across the northern states — whites, blacks, boys, girls — all students who had given up their summer to work in Mississippi. In some parts of the state they had built makeshift schools and set up health clinics, but mostly they were here to get people registered to vote. He said they sometimes moved from county to county, depending on the need, but I suspected that staying on the move was in their best interests for safety reasons as well.

In their absence, Mr. Townsend led the meetings, but, to my surprise, it was Graden who was responsible for most of the organizing. He weaved through the barn, shaking hands and addressing each person, reassuring those he sensed were weakening, reasoning with those who suggested last-minute changes to the plans. Despite his youth, it was obvious that he was held in high regard. He carried himself with the same confident air that had struck me when I saw the young northerner grab the crowd. In those few hours, in Mr. Townsend's barn in the middle of the night, I saw that my brother had become much more than what our father had feared.

Our bus was one of six, rented with funds donated by a student group at a northern state college as well as with money collected by our church. The breeze through the windows kept us cool while we were moving, but at each stop the heat smothered us in its grip. Some of the men were dripping sweat, but no one seemed to care. The bus rang with church standards and old field songs.

Graden was the youngest among us. At just a few weeks shy of his eighteenth birthday he was unable to vote, but that didn't deter him from throwing his energy into this voter registration rally, attending meetings with the northern students, canvassing houses to speak to people about their rights and why they must exercise them, and holding education sessions in the back room of the church. I couldn't believe that he had found the time to do so much and keep it hidden from the family, but he told me that he had been skipping out of school, several days a week. On those nights when he stayed up late to teach me, we did lessons that he had made up himself.

The bus driver told Graden that the drive to Jackson would take about an hour and a quarter. We were forty-five minutes in before I began to get nervous. I had never been this far from home, and while the others sang, I stared out the window. We rolled slowly by shallow swamps, the trees tangling amongst each other and occasionally dripping leaves on to the still, moss-covered water; past clapboard and tar-paper shacks, jumbled together and haphazardly placed within a few feet of the rust-coloured gravel road; then over the tracks and turning on to the plantation-flanked highway, row upon row of cotton just beginning to burst from its bolls and long driveways leading to the gates of antebellum mansions; and finally into the outer edges of Jackson.

If I leaned my head out a little, I could hear shouting and snatches of song carried on the wind from the bus ahead of us. Graden sat quietly beside me, beaming. His leg bounced up and down in time with the singing. I elbowed him playfully to get his attention. He smiled and placed his hand on my arm.

"I'm glad you came."

"I only came to look out for you."

Graden laughed. "You go ahead and tell yourself that. Whatever the reason, you are here. And together we're gonna change things." He gestured around the bus. "All of us, together, are gonna change things."

"The only thing that's gonna change is that look on your face when we get home, and Ma and Pa find out where we've been."

"That's your problem, Warren. That's Daddy's problem. That's so many people's problem: they are only thinking about the small things. This is bigger than that, brother. This is a chance for us to stand up and tell everyone that we will not be looked down on."

"Humph. A whupping from Daddy ain't no small thing. And you got all these crazy ..."

The rhythm of the singing broke, and the bus slowed. Graden stood and looked out the window opposite him. He called up to the bus driver.

"We're not supposed to stop here."

The driver shrugged and gestured towards the road ahead. The other buses had stopped in front of him. Graden crawled over me and stood in the aisle, trying to make out what was going on.

Others were standing now as well, looking out the windows and whispering. There was the slow clomp of hooves on pavement as police on horseback flanked the sides of the row of buses. They moved without urgency. The horses' heads were as high as the bus windows, but the blinders they wore kept them looking straight ahead. The men astride them were calm, but wore full equipment — vests, helmets, visors.

Graden moved down the aisle to the front of the bus. The driver slid the door open, but before Graden could get off, a state trooper had dismounted and was stepping onto the bus.

"Back to your seat."

"Sir, we are on our way to Jackson to exercise our right to vote."

"I said back to your seat."

Graden was a half-head taller than the officer. He stood straight and showed no signs of budging, though he was careful to keep his arms at his sides and not appear aggressive. The officer looked past him and addressed the rest of the bus.

"Everyone sit down. You're going to have to turn these buses around and go home. It's too dangerous."

"We are not afraid of danger, sir, and we will not turn around. We are on our way to Jackson. We intend to be peaceful, and we intend to exercise our rights. We have every confidence that the police of this state will protect us from any threats."

I winced at the words, torn between pride and fear. Graden looked and sounded for all the world like the sharp young northerner who had originally stoked these people's courage, but this wasn't the north and staring down a policeman here had only one outcome. I could feel the tension throughout the bus, and I hoped that these people would not back down, that they would stand with Graden. I hoped their courage would hold, and that mine would as well. The trooper took off his sunglasses and looked at Graden wearily.

"Son, there's a whole lot of angry people in the street up ahead of you, and I don't think they mean to be peaceful at all. So you're going to have to turn around."

"We will not, sir. We have a right to continue on, and if there are people who intend to stop us by force, then it is the responsibility of the law to control those people."

"Now, you listen here! I ain't gonna stand here and have some boy tell me how to do my job. I'm not here to protect you, I'm here to keep the peace, and if …"

He was cut off by shouts from outside. A crowd of white protesters were encircling the buses, some carrying signs, others carrying baseball bats, bricks, and stones. The bus began rock-ing as they pushed against the sides, slapping angrily at the win-dows. The trooper gave Graden a look that said "I warned you" and exited without another word. I watched as the crowd parted in front of him to let him through.

I went to the front and grabbed Graden by the shoulder.

"We shouldn't be here!" I cursed myself for not having more sense, for not having listened to Papa. I thought protecting Graden meant coming along with him, but there was no way to protect him here. I had failed the moment I let him get on the bus. Running was the only thing that made sense to me, but there was nowhere to run, and besides I knew Graden wouldn't follow me.

Graden shook off my hand and tried to calm the passengers, urging them to stay away from the windows. We heard glass shat-ter, and suddenly there was dark smoke billowing from the win-dows of the bus ahead of us. The emergency back door opened, and people clamoured to get out, screaming and beating at their burning clothes. The crowd grabbed them as they exited and threw them to the ground, kicking, punching, and swinging wildly.

One woman on our bus dashed for the door, but Graden grabbed her and held her back. He yelled for everyone to lay down in the aisle. Before doing so, I looked again out the window, and be-hind the throng of angry faces, I saw a dozen or more state troopers lined up, sitting calmly atop their horses and doing nothing.

I crouched in the aisle with the rest and waited for a firebomb to claim our bus as well. I could hear the slurs and shouts. A window crashed, and I looked up, but it was only a brick, bouncing off the opposite wall of the bus and finally coming to rest on the dirty floor. Then there was a loud banging, and the bus shuddered even more violently than before. The crowd were using their bats and clubs to smash the sides of our bus. The rear sank down as they cut the tires.

I looked at Graden, but there was no trace of fear. All I could see was disappointment.

◄ ►

The state troopers let the crowd have their way for a few terrifying minutes before stepping in. A shot was fired in the air, and a trooper called out orders over bullhorn for the crowd to disperse. Once they were under control, we were led off the buses and told to lay face-down on the hot asphalt. The hooves of the troopers' horses clacked heavily near our faces. We were cuffed and led to state police cars in small groups.

"You are all under arrest for disturbing the peace. I will not stand for the inciting of riots in this state ..."

"We didn't do anything," someone shouted. An officer pulled the man up by one arm and clubbed him half-heartedly behind the ear before dragging him off.

We spent the night packed fifteen to a cell in cells intended for two. We huddled close together to make room for the wounded to sit. A woman in my cell sniffled faintly while pulling remnants of cloth from a patch of burned skin on her arm. Her eyes were glazed and distant. Others had wide cuts and scrapes and ugly, swollen lumps. One man's forearm was violently crooked, and he held his wrist in his lap while resting his head against the bars.

Some cried, or shook, or murmured. An older woman tried to sing, but no one joined in and her voice soon faltered. There were calls for help and calls for arms, angry speeches shouted out, and just as quickly shouted down or shouted over, but when Graden finally spoke, they stayed quiet.

"We knew this could happen. You all knew this risk and you came anyway, and I am proud of you all, but we are just beginning. They use their dogs and their fire and their clubs against us because their *ideas* have lost their force. And so they turn to force. But if we yield to these tactics, they will continue to use them. If we let them push us back then they will continue to push us. The way to defeat them is simply not to be deterred. Not to be intimidated. To show them that the power they wield will not give them power over us."

He continued, but I can't remember all that he said. I was transfixed by the serenity on his face, the poise in his manner, the inability of the environment to influence him, and the inability of the others to resist. He stood with the grace of command.

He soothed them and rallied them at the same time. He convinced them that action would be taken, but not violent action. "We will resist these injustices, not with force but with our persistence. We will frustrate those who oppose us with our refusal to quit. We have placed a stake in the ground today, and we cannot allow anyone to move it."

The guards outside the row of cells had been content to stay there when the crowd was riled up, but the calmness unsettled them. They came and stood by the door of Graden's cell, but he continued to speak. As the group murmured their support, the guards fidgeted and shot sideways glances at each other. They went back outside and switched off the lights. We stood together in utter darkness. They cut the fans as well, and the heat filled the spaces between us. My clothes stuck to my chest and shoulders and sweat ran down my face like a sheet. I heard the gasping of hot air as some laboured to breathe and felt the shifting of the crowd as people tried to get closer to the bars to find relief.

We stayed that way throughout the night. In the morning we were led out of our cells three at a time, driven out to the edge of the city, and dropped off at the side of the road without a word, left to find our own way back. I was in one of the first cars, and I waited on the shoulder while the state cars pulled up time after time until finally they brought Graden. He stepped out of the car with dignity, as if he had been politely offered a ride, and I saw in him the victory of which he'd spoken: a victory achieved solely by not allowing himself to feel defeated.

12

AMBLAN, 2008

THE STORM CAME IN THE NIGHT like an old dream. The snow and the dark fell in concert across Amblan. The streetlights came on as if in warning, but the flakes fluttered past, at first large and lazy and soft, then as the wind picked up, fast and sharp. The town was typically quiet after dark, but the few people who were caught outside pulled their hoods tight against the sting of sleet and headed to the comfort of their homes. By morning, the snow had taken the town. Eight fresh inches rested on what had already accumulated. It had blown in from the east and it hung moss-like off the side of every tree, signpost, and parking meter. Trucks parked along the side streets had been swallowed up except for one headlight, and one side door, and still the snow continued to fall.

I rolled over, banging my elbow against the wall, and woke, disoriented. I had moved the bed to the far corner of the room, away from the cracked window. I rubbed my elbow and went over to look through the glass, wrapping the sheets around me. My bare feet slapped against the wood floor. The wind made a sharp whistling sound as it pushed through the crack, and I could feel the cold of it as I peered out over the desk.

My right hand ached, and I flexed it absentmindedly, trying to warm it. After I was showered and dressed, I went downstairs to fix coffee. The forecast on the radio called for more snow with no expectation of it letting up for days. Schools were open, but were expected to close early, and snowploughs were working around the clock to clear the streets. If the lady in the coffee shop was right, the roads into the hills would soon be impassable. I poured the rest of the coffee into a thermos.

It had snowed and melted and snowed again, creating treacherous conditions. The surface was almost blue and reflected the weak sunlight in soft and crystalline hues. It crunched under my boots, but beneath the upper crust the snow was soft enough to sink clean through to the bottom. Each time I took a step, I had to lift my leg back up to free it from the nearly perfect footprint. I walked to the parking lot that way, my arms out to the side as I shifted back and forth to maintain my balance, like slogging through a mud-soaked field, hunched over between the rows of cotton.

The parking lot had been cleared except for a thin sheet of packed and tire-rutted snow, and when I reached it, my legs felt suddenly light. I unplugged the block heater from the post and let the cord retract until only its plug hung out from the grill, lolling there like the tongue of a friendly dog. I started the Explorer, then started scraping the ice from the windows. By the time I got in the vehicle, my arms and legs burned with the effort from the short trek through the deep drifts.

There were very few cars. Most of the vehicles I passed were SUVs or oversized pickup trucks with roof-mounted lights and gun-racks on the cab. The traffic had turned the streets a slushy brown, and the bottom third of every vehicle, moving or parked, was marked with the same colour.

I pulled out the card on which I'd scribbled all of Etta's contact information. The post office attendant watched me curiously while I faxed the photo. When the fax confirmation printed out, I crumpled the sheet, put it in my pocket, and left, bypassing the garbage can by the door.

In the Explorer, I pulled out a notebook from my satchel and flipped to a roughly sketched map that I'd made of the town, studying it as I sipped coffee from the thermos. Earl Daniel's house was more than two miles outside of town, but the drive was probably about six miles, due to the way the road wound through the hills and brush, at one point dropping down to a single lane with the occasional turnout where cars could pull off to let oncoming cars pass. I looked out the window at the fresh snow that was already starting to fall and guessed that the road would probably not be open for much longer. I took one more look at the map, then set the notebook down on the passenger seat and turned the key in the ignition.

◄ ►

I edged the rented SUV up through the hills, focussed on the road ahead. The storm had reduced the road to a column of hard-packed snow, lined with parallel tracks of brown slush, marking the treads where previous cars had passed. The snow still appeared to be falling heavily, but it was impossible to tell how much of it was fresh and how much was being blown off the stands of evergreens that flanked the road. The snow swirled violently in front of my vehicle, and the gusts of wind were strong enough at times that I could feel their impact as they struck against the doors. The windshield wipers offered conical and intermittent glimpses of the path ahead.

I hunched over the steering wheel and before long my back ached with the strain, but I stayed in that position. Even then, I could only make out dark shapes in the shifting white curtain in front of me, unable to distinguish their source until I was almost directly upon them. I came upon a pickup truck that had missed the bend in the road and plunged into a short ditch beneath a bank of trees. The front half and the cab of the truck had been nearly engulfed. The bed was tilted, one rear tire rested on the edge of the road, the other suspended. The word *Ford* was still visible on the tailgate, and the right taillight blinked, as if it were a street sign pointing the way towards the town of Ford. The two muddy lines that had marked the road stopped at that point, and I had to navigate the rest of the way simply by keeping my vehicle centered between the trees.

The ridges of the hard-packed snow pushed the tires left and right, and the softer snow collecting on the surface provided little purchase with which to stop the skidding. I veered along the centre of the road as if I were crashing into invisible bumpers on either side that kept pushing me back to the middle. It required such concentration that I almost drove past the posts marking the entrance to Earl Daniel's driveway.

13

MISSISSIPPI, 1964

ONE OTHER THING happened that summer that had consequences, both immediate and lasting.

Seeing Graden stand calmly in the midst of the prison, seeing how the older people responded to him, seeing him step proudly out of the back of the state car: all these things inspired me immensely in the moment. But later at night, lying safely back in my bed and staring at the familiar criss-crossed beams in the ceiling, they troubled me.

My worries were twofold. First, there was the simple matter of safety. The warning my father had issued after the cotton-selling incident continued to play in the back of my mind. About the value of prudence. About the danger of courage. About survival. I knew now, though, that there was very little that I could do to protect Graden. He had chosen a path, and he had committed himself to it completely.

That led to my second worry. There was doubt in my mind as to whether or not I wanted to be a part of this. I felt the same stirrings of passion when Graden and the others spoke, the same anger at the rights and freedoms that had been denied us, and the same thrill at the glimpses they offered of a more optimistic future. But I lacked Graden's surety of purpose, and I knew that this would always be so. This cause was his, not mine.

Graden and the others continued to meet after the failed rally, and I continued to go, but not as regularly and not with the same conviction. I never wanted to be on that bus again, never wanted to be in the midst of that mob. I told myself that Papa was right, that it was just common sense, but in my heart I knew that it was fear. I couldn't bring myself to face those people because I felt that that they would look at me and know I was afraid.

Graden would get up in the darkness and wait for me to join him, but more and more often I would stay behind, and after he'd slipped away, I would get up and cross the woods to the gin shack at the top of the hill.

The shack was a small, abandoned grain shed when we had found it. The floor was filthy with bits of rotted corn and old mice droppings. We had scrubbed the floor clean and sanded the inside walls. We did not want to attract attention by changing the outside appearance too much, but we replaced a handful of the most damaged boards. We cut up old pallets and staked them down over the floor to make it a more level surface, but there were wide seams between the planks at some points, and at the end of a night of dancing, almost everyone was coated from the knees down in spilled drink and dust. The roof was composed of overlapping sheets of corrugated metal nailed onto crooked beams, and it pushed the music down onto us like a scratchy echo.

It was three boys and me to begin with — the Tittle brothers, Sam and Ronnie, and their cousin, John Young. A few more had become regulars since then. It was John who invited Faye Raigan, who in turn invited two of her friends, Sandra and Nancy. Before long we had a pretty decent crowd. We set up a couple of tables that we had salvaged from scrap, and we built a simple pine bar.

On a typical night, Sam and Ronnie would bring in two or three jugs of homemade gin, John would set up his radio and fiddle with the antenna until he could pick up something danceable, and one of the other boys would come rolling in with two girls on his arms, as if the old grain shed were the Cotton Club itself. We would sit at the bar and listen to music, take turns dancing with the girls, or sit at the tables and play cards, sipping gin and trying not to make sour faces at the taste. There would be others present from time to time as well, but generally they were friends or family or someone who had been invited by one of the core group.

On rare occasions a stranger would show up, based solely on having heard that a good time was to be had, but we treated those people warily and they usually left disappointed. It was during that last summer that Penny Newcome walked in.

She was a sliver of moonlight in the doorway, thin and pale. Strands of her long blond hair fell in front and behind her ears. She wasn't a true beauty, but she moved with an alluring confidence, her mouth parted suggestively, her wiry frame and heavy breasts exuded sex.

There were two friends as well, but they stood back, huddled meekly behind her. No one spoke when she entered. The others looked around, then looked at their feet, but I couldn't take my eyes away, and maybe that's why she chose me. She waited for a moment in the doorway, peered into the makeshift hall, then smiled giddily, and strolled into the room. She chewed on her bottom lip and continued to soak in her surroundings with a strange kind of awe while the hem of her dotted dress swayed about her knees. Ronnie and Sam had been on the dance floor with Faye, but they stepped aside and pressed themselves to the walls.

Penny's friends entered more hesitantly, holding each other by the arm. One of them called Penny's name in a harsh whisper, but Penny just smiled and trailed her finger along the top of the bar. She turned to look at me, and I felt locked in place. I was drunk, but not so drunk that I was unafraid. I simply could not look away. The truth is, I wanted her to choose me. There was a part of me that wanted her to choose anyone but me, but in the hungriest part of my soul, I didn't care about the risk.

She sat down beside me on the knotted bench. Her eyes were dull with whiskey. I could smell it on her as well, but beneath that there was a citrusy scent that urged me to lean closer. She curled the loose hair back behind her ear, and I could see the smooth plane of her neck. I wanted to put my lips on it and taste the saltiness of her skin. I finally looked away, searching the room for help, but there was none. I stood up, and she stood up with me. She was a small girl, the top of her head barely reaching my chin.

"You shouldn't be here, Miss." My throat was a desert, and each word was a stone dragged across its cracking surface.

"From what I hear, your parties are a little more fun than ours. What's your name?"

"Warren."

"Well, Warren, do you dance?"

Sam slid behind her and glanced at me over her shoulder, the warning clear in his eyes. She put her hand on my chest. I swallowed hard and reached for her. I moved stiffly at first, trying to minimize the contact. I could feel every set of eyes on me — my friends lined up along the bar and the back wall, tense and rigid; her friends, hovering just inside the doorway, uncertain and ready to flee.

Penny pressed up on her toes and whispered to me, "Not like that. Dance with me like you dance with them."

My hand was a dark stain on her upper arm. Her short, shallow breaths fluttered against my collarbone, and I closed my eyes. I felt the tension in my shoulders slide away beneath her touch. I twirled her and swung her back close to me. I moved my hand to her hip. It felt different. Not meaty and powerful like the girls I had danced with before, but supple and elegant. Fragile. A bone carving moving rhythmically against my palm. Seductive rather than aggressive.

I focussed just on the music and on her. Her ankles were already patterned with dust. She dipped her head then rolled it back, revealing again the swath of smooth skin along her neck and collarbone. The length of her hair fell across the back of my hand as I held her and sent a charge up my entire arm. I felt myself growing hard, but I couldn't pull away from her. She turned to me, her shoulders against my chest, my hands on her waist, her blond hair beneath my chin. I breathed deep, taking in all of her that I could. Then the music stopped.

John stood by the radio, his hand still on the button. The eyes that had been on us now turned away.

"Penny."

Her friends were still only a few feet from the doorway, having never moved from that spot.

"Penny, I think we should leave."

◄ ►

On the way home that night, I slipped off the side of road to the spongy underbrush to masturbate. I spilled myself against the base of a withered pine tree, urgent and awkward, face flushed with the shame of the act and the memory of Penny's body pressed against mine.

The relief allowed me to finally think clearly, and I ran through scenarios in my mind of what would happen if she or her friends ever told anyone. Every black boy in Mississippi knew about Emmett Till, the fourteen-year-old from Chicago who had whistled at a white girl while visiting family here in Mississippi and was later found in the Tallahatchie River with a seventy-pound cotton gin fan tied around his neck with barb wire. I'd done far more than whistle. By the time I reached home, I was crazed with fear and furious at my carelessness. I worked the field the next day, glancing over my shoulder every few minutes, expecting to see a pickup appear carrying an angry father or brother. My distractedness did not go unnoticed, by either Graden or my father, though neither would ever guess at the cause.

Although it was never talked about, by then Papa knew that we were sneaking out at night — Graden to attend meetings and me to drink cheap gin — and he disapproved equally of both of us. He would glare at us each morning, daring us to look back at him. Then we would eat breakfast while Mama, Glenda, and Etta chatted cheerily to try to raise the mood, and Papa, Graden, and I were silent.

I stayed away from the gin shack for several weeks after the dance with Penny, but I avoided Graden's meetings as well. On the nights that he edged his way out of the bedroom and across the backyard, I would conjure Penny again, the two of us alone this time in the old shack, my hand sliding up beneath her dress, feeling the firmness of her milky inner thigh, hooking my fingers around the band of her cotton panties ...

I returned to the gin shack after a while, but when I was there, every noise, every stray headlight, added an additional beat to my heart. Instead of dancing and laughing, I sat quietly in the corner, drinking. Before I would come home buzzed and slightly tired, but now I was coming home roaring drunk. Not tiptoeing but singing and shouting as I stumbled through the backyard and into the hallway, daring someone to say something. Once, I did not come home at all. I woke in the morning on the shack's sticky floor, ants crawling across my chest and legs.

Graden was outside the shack, sitting on a rock.

"Figured this is where you'd be."

"You here to rescue me, then?"

"From what? Ants?" Graden laughed, and I brushed the ants and dirt off my clothes. I shielded my eyes from the brightness of the sun.

"I guess I must be a sight."

"Sure are."

"What'd you tell Papa?"

"They don't know you're gone. I had Etta fake sick. She

wailed and moaned and begged for Mama and Papa to take her into town to see the doctor. She might be an actress, that one."

"Glenda?"

"Well, she didn't think you were worth all the trouble, but she won't squeal. I hope you're ready for a long day of work. Papa's still expecting the field to get hoe'd, and I ain't doing your share."

"You remember when I used to do yours? When you were sneaking off to school?"

Graden smiled. "I remember. But I'm not paying you back to come here. Told you this place was no good."

"You just say that 'cause you don't know how to have fun. You can't dance like me." I teased. I tapped out a few exaggerated steps in the heat, snapping my fingers and watching Graden laugh.

"You're going to be doing some real dancing if Papa finds out you slept here. You better hope Etta's the actress I think she is. Come on."

He put his arm around my shoulder. We walked home together that day, and from then on Graden came to fetch me every Tuesday night, showing up at the shack after his own secret meetings were done, sometimes half-pulling me along the road as I stumbled beside him.

Each time we walked past the old pine that marked the half-way point between the shack and home, I thought about Penny Newcome. I didn't know anyone else who had danced with a white girl, and there was a little pride in that. I wanted to tell Graden, but I knew he would just think it was trouble.

When the trouble did come, it was not a father or a brother, as I had feared, but a boyfriend.

◄ ►

Mama was prepping her fruits and vegetables like she did at the end of every summer, preserving some in water and salt, pickling or stewing others, or turning some into jams. Glenda and Etta worked with her as she cut, peeled, pressed, and stirred, filling the kitchen with an overpowering sweetness. She slid a couple of dollars into my hand and asked me to go in to town to get her a few more jars. Mama sometimes got an extra dollar or two from the white families that she cleaned for, and she would hide the money away in a rolled-up apron in the cupboard, kept for just such expenses, a secret about as poorly kept as our late-night excursions.

I drove our old truck into town, parking it close to Greely's grocery store, where I found what I needed as quickly as possible. Greely was a stern-looking man, with a hard jaw and dark hair streaked with grey, face pock-marked from long-forgotten acne. He never took his eyes off me. I took the jars to the counter and slid the money towards him, careful to keep my eyes down. He handed me a bag in which to carry the jars, and I exited the store into the dusty street.

On the other side of the road, three young white men milled about outside the service station, drinking cokes and leaning against the freezer outside the door. One of them was talking to a slim, dark-haired girl in a flowered dress. Our eyes met, and I recognized her as one of Penny's reticent friends from the gin shack. She stopped mid-sip, the bottle held just short of her mouth. We stared at each other from across the street. The man she was talking to turned his head to see what she was looking at. I hugged the grocery bag high and tight to my chest with both arms, trying to cover my face, then headed towards the truck as quickly as I could without drawing any attention to myself.

I heard a shout coming from behind me, but kept walking. Heard the slap of running feet against the sun-baked ground, felt a hand on my shoulder, spinning me. I fell to the ground and the bag slipped from my hands, crashing in front of me. The three of them stood over me. I remember the smell of hair gel and cologne, the brightness of light reflected off the shards of broken glass jars, the tightening of skin at the back of my head as a hand pulled me by the hair. Breath in my face, hot and threatening, then a dull thud, and the taste of blood. Rustling of pant legs, flurry of boots, pain in my ribs, my back, my groin. My own hands in front of my face like shadows.

"Is this the one? This the one that put his hands on Penny?"

The girl covered her face with her hands. Her shoulders shook with sobbing, but she still looked at me and nodded.

"Bring him over to the truck."

I was dragged over to the gas station. The boy shouting instructions removed his jacket. He tossed it into the back of his truck, then lowered the tailgate. He turned and punched me hard in the jaw. I went limp, slumping backwards.

"Hold him up. You want to touch my girlfriend? Huh? Huh? Grab his hand."

They pressed my hand against the back of the truck, just above the taillight. The boy who punched me grabbed the tailgate and slammed it upwards. The pain brought me back into focus. My leg twitched, drawing a half-moon in the dirt. My head lolled. I bit my tongue and felt fresh blood on my chin. He shouted something at me, then the gate slammed again, and I felt it like a thump in my chest. A twist of the boy's thickly gelled hair had come loose at the front, swinging wildly about his now-sweating forehead. His mouth was pressed closed, the lips thin and white. His eyes were in shadow, as if they had sunken deeper into their sockets. The gate slammed once more, then he stepped back, panting, reaching up to put the rebellious lock of hair back into place. The arms beneath me let go, and I fell to the ground, curling up and bringing my arm in against my chest. The dark-haired girl was crying in the doorway of the service station. Before the boys got in the truck to drive away, one of them went back for his Coke.

14

CHICAGO, 1965

A FEW WEEKS AFTER Graden's funeral, I packed up and headed north. No one tried to stop me. Mama unfurled the apron in the cupboard and gave me everything she had saved up, a total of seventeen dollars, but she didn't argue against my going.

The money was enough for bus fare to Chicago. I sat by the window. I wouldn't look at any of the other passengers. Instead I watched as the landscapes rolled past — Tennessee, Kentucky, Indiana — places I had never expected to see. I remember little. I stepped off the bus into the cool Chicago air and felt my skin constrict. I had never owned a jacket. It was early morning when I arrived, not yet light out, and I pulled what few clothes I had out of my bag and covered myself with them so that I could sleep a few hours, huddled against the station wall.

I walked the city by day, starting by the waterfront and working my way out further and further in exploratory circles, then returning each night to the relative safety of the bus station to sleep. The station master woke me once, cap in hand and a stern look on his face. I could see the words ready to form on his lips to send me away or possibly to call the police, but after staring at me for a few moments, he placed his cap back on his head and walked off. It was the first act of kindness that I had been shown by a white man, and I slept that night without fear for the first time in a long time.

When I woke up, there was a piece of paper curled inside my shirt pocket, with a name and the address of a northside diner.

I was dirty and tired when I entered the restaurant, bag in hand. The owner looked at the note, studied me, then nodded for me to come around the back.

"You're a southerner?"

"Yes, sir."

"You ever work in a restaurant before?"

"No, sir. I can read, though, and I know some math."

The owner wiped his forehead and laughed.

"Well, none of that is going to help you much here." He looked at my gnarled right hand. "Can you hold a mop with that?"

He brought me in through the kitchen and put me to work washing dishes and mopping the floors and bathrooms. At the end of the shift, he gave me directions to a shelter. It was the first time I'd slept in a bed other than the crooked wood-framed cot back home in Mississippi. I woke in the middle of the night and listened to the sounds of the men resting in the darkness around me. I had never been so lonely. I looked across at the spot where Graden would have been sleeping, but in his place was a grizzled and sickly thin man in a tank top. I pulled a journal and a pencil from my bag and angled myself into the moonlight to practice the mathematics that he'd taught me.

I wanted to thank the station master for his kindness, but I never went back. I continued walking the city in the mornings, then working at the diner afternoons and evenings. I stole books. I picked them up from café patios when people left them at an unwatched table or forgot them on buses or park benches. I read them at the diner at night whenever the owner stepped out, or I pulled the journal from my waistband and scribbled out problems.

One night, a man tapped me on the shoulder while I was mopping. It was early, and I was rushing to get the floor cleaned before the supper crowd came in.

"I think you dropped this."

I turned to see a man holding my journal. He was about my height, but thin. In his sweat pants and loose sweater, he looked more slovenly than athletic. I guessed he was probably about Papa's age, but his years had not been as hard as Papa's. He didn't have the creased skin, the greying hair, the stoop from years of hard labour. The man extended the journal towards me, his hand trembling as he did so.

"Thank you."

"You're welcome. I made a few notations. I hope you don't mind. It was open," he added hastily. "I didn't pry."

I opened the journal, and he showed me where he had made corrections. The tremor in his hands was more pronounced as he traced the figures across the page.

"Are you a math student?"

I laughed off his question and lifted my mop. "No, sir. I'm a floor washer."

"Well, for a floor washer, you're pretty good with numbers. Who taught you math?"

I gripped the mop tighter and looked at the floor. I thought of Graden often of course, but it was when he came up unexpectedly that his absence hit me the most. I exhaled and muttered something about getting back to work.

"OK," the man said. "But if you want to keep learning, you should call me. I'm Tim. Tim Barnes. You've done well, and I'm guessing you've done it mostly on your own. Everybody needs a little help sometimes."

He scribbled his number in my notebook, gave me a brief smile, and returned to his table. I laid in the bed at the shelter that night, going over the corrections. I wanted Graden to be there to show me where I'd gone wrong. I pictured Graden's writing on the page; Graden's fingers going over the figures; Graden's voice explaining the error.

Two days later, I called Mr. Barnes from a pay phone, and he invited me to come see him, giving me directions to his house. I was still wary of white people, but he seemed completely harmless.

His house was a plain brick duplex a few blocks from Lakeshore. He welcomed me in and offered me a slice of meatloaf and a baked potato. I thanked him, and he apologized for not having something more.

"I used to be quite the cook," he said. "Even before my wife passed, I was always the one to make dinner."

He held up his shaking hands and smiled wistfully. "It's getting harder though."

"What's wrong with your hands?"

"Palsy," he replied. "I have good days and bad days, but lately even the good days are not so good. And your hand?"

I pretended to chew while I considered how to answer.

"I made a mistake."

"I see. Well, I hope you find Chicago more … forgiving."

He raised his glass, and I was thankful he didn't press for details. I cleaned the dishes after our meal and put them away in the cupboard. He laid out textbooks on the kitchen table. His hands sometimes locked so that he could barely turn the pages, but he tutored me in math, science, and literature, much like Graden had. At first I only visited occasionally. Then I began going to his house more and more often, cleaning the yard, clearing the eavestroughs, and performing whatever chores he couldn't do himself, although my own crippled hand was often scarcely more useful than his.

I told him about life in the South, about growing up on the farm, and about leaving Mississippi to come north, but I never mentioned Graden and he never pushed me for more than what I was willing to tell him. After a few months, I moved out of the shelter and into his basement. He arranged for me to attend classes at the high school where he taught. I graduated at the age of twenty-nine.

I enrolled in college with the money that I'd saved from my job at the diner. It wasn't enough, but my history was. The dean gave me special dispensation to attend.

I excelled at my courses, but avoided social contact as much as possible. I was the only southerner on campus, and the wide-eyed and idealistic young men and women, mostly black, but some liberal-minded whites as well, wanted to know what it was "really like" in Mississippi. I thought of Graden, standing in the Townsends' barn, lit by lanterns and encouraging an uncertain crowd of farmers and labourers to exercise their rights. I thought of the northerner in the brand-new coveralls that everyone looked at reverentially while he spoke of things he knew nothing about, and I knew now where his kind came from. I wanted nothing to do with any of them.

I cultivated an isolationist persona, a deeply ingrained separateness. I would offer argument to any opinion, even to one I agreed with. I feigned indifference to the other students' activities and blocked off any potentially probing conversations by simply shrugging and grunting, rather than giving real responses. I didn't simply withdraw from people; I aggressively pushed them away.

The students watched grainy footage of James Meredith entering Ole Miss under armed guard. They watched fire hoses and dogs turned on children. They stood in school halls and the courtyard and the cafeteria and shouted about injustice and about fighting to support their "brothers and sisters in the South," and they couldn't understand why I wouldn't stand beside them. They began to whisper behind my back that I was a traitor and a coward. They finally began to avoid me like I avoided them. They held the most perverse of jealousies against me: they envied my suffering.

I listened to them speak and looked at their faces and felt certain that they knew nothing about Mississippi. The ones who went down on buses to "help the cause," came back quiet, stunned. I saw the same look years later on the faces of those white boys returning from Vietnam. They left convinced of their own invulnerability and sense of right, with dreams of glory, service, and heroism, and they came back having learned far too much about the world. The world is not a place of theory, not a place of ideas. It is a concrete slab that is cold, hard, and unyielding.

◄ ►

I met Anne in the college library. It was the way she moved that first caught my attention, an effortless gracefulness while she floated down the aisle, trailing the tips of her fingers across the spines of the books as if offering them her blessing. She wore a long cotton dress, grass-green, tied tight around her waist, and alternately clinging and loosening about her knees and thighs, offering a glimpse of her form, then taking it away. She seemed to move just a fraction more slowly than everyone else in the room, as if she knew that the world would wait for her.

She tilted her head and smiled, then walked over to the table where I was reading and sat down, across from me. She was an array of colours — kinked black hair flowing over caramel skin, studying me with water-blue eyes.

"Do you like jazz?" she asked.

I had grown up listening to the country station out of Hattiesburg. I had heard a few jazz standards at the gin shack, but for the most part I had no idea what it was. I nodded anyway.

"Good," she said. "Otherwise this will never work."

"What won't?"

She smiled again. "I don't think people can ever really love each other. But they can share a love for common things."

She stood and walked away without another word. It took me two weeks to learn her name, and another week before I was able to find her again. I spent hours in the jazz section of the library. I scoured nearby blues joints hoping for another glimpse of her. I visited record stores and finally found her working at one, just off campus. I spent most of the meagre amount of money I had saved on records by Sonny Rollins and Charlie Parker. She played them for me in the store, and she swayed slightly behind the counter while we spoke, making it hard for me to concentrate on her words.

"They say that Coltrane sometimes practices until his gums bleed. Can you imagine that? Having that kind of commitment to something?"

I pictured the criss-crossing scars on my father's arms as he smoked on the porch, Graden being lowered into the ground, his remains rattling against the side of the coffin. Bleeding gums seemed an easy sacrifice, but I nodded anyway, mesmerized by how deeply moved she could be.

I spent all the time I could with her. I was still working at the diner, but I ran home after each shift to clean up, spending any tips I'd earned taking her to hear jazz in smoke-filled clubs. When we didn't have money, we would sit outside on the sidewalk and listen to the music streaming through the doors and into the street.

Anne was something I had never encountered before. I'd known people who lived simple lives, and if they had a passion for something, like Graden, that passion was focussed towards one end. Anne was worldly, and her energy was not harnessed by any one interest. She spoke Spanish and German and sometimes teased me with words I couldn't comprehend. She drew incessantly in a spiral-bound sketchbook that she carried with her at all times. Besides music, she taught me about art and literature, making my own math studies seem dull by comparison. She sometimes stopped in the middle of a conversation to make grand proclamations.

"Sometimes I think that the world's problems could be prevented if you could get the right book to the right person at the right time."

"How so?" I asked.

"What if Stalin had read Sartre instead of Marx? What if Hitler had read Neruda or Gabriela Mistral?"

"It wouldn't change anything," I said. "It would just make them well-read dictators."

We were sitting on the curb in front of a coffee shop, and she threw a balled up napkin at me.

"That's your problem, Warren. You have no imagination. You look at the world and see what it is, instead of what it could be."

"People die trying to figure out what the world could be. People survive by accepting what it is."

She pouted playfully and crossed her arms.

"If everyone had your attitude, things would never change."

"Maybe they never will."

Halfway through my first year, Mr. Barnes passed away. Anne was ready to console me, but it wasn't necessary. I had become close to him, but I understood loss in a way Anne couldn't, and I moved on.

I found a place in a hostel near campus, and Anne moved a few of her belongings in as well. We laid face to face in the dark and whispered to one another. While I told her little about my past, she told me everything about hers. She offered her childhood up to me in great detail along with her opinions about everything from political issues to the quality of the soup that I brought home from the diner. She seemingly gave voice to any random thought that strayed through her mind, and I absorbed it all, fascinated, while carefully sharing nothing in return.

◀ ▶

During this period, I had the same brutal dream, night after night.

I was sitting on a bench in Jackson Park, looking out over Lake Michigan. The waves lapped gently at the shore break. There was a man on the bench beside me, throwing out bits of corn. Seagulls circled overhead, but none were drawn by his offering. Instead, a single crow pecked about on the pavement, picking up the kernels one by one. It hopped about awkwardly, as if its wing were injured. I could not see the face of the man beside me.

Another man strode down the path towards us. He was wearing hard, polished boots, jeans, and a plain white T-shirt. His hair was straight and black and slicked back with oil. He lifted the stranger off the bench beside me and pushed him down onto the sidewalk. He asked questions that I could never quite make out, though the two men were right in front of me. He kicked the stranger in the ribs, then brought the hard black boots down twice on his head.

Others appeared, joining in on the attack. I tried to get up to help the stranger, but I couldn't move. I felt the ache in my crippled right hand, and it pinned me to the bench. Pain ripped down the scar on the back just as intensely as it had while it was being slammed over and over in the tailgate of the truck.

I listened to the cold crack of the stranger's skull against the pavement, the snapping of bones as the men mercilessly kicked and stamped on him. Their shoes and the hems of their pants were speckled with blood. The man on the ground never cried out, but always he reached for me, fingers outstretched in silent pleading. I never got up from the bench. Afterwards, one of the attackers would turn to me and smile.

The dreams would wake me in the middle of the night, but not with a jolt. I would arrive at a dulled state of half-consciousness and stare at the ceiling, disturbed and ashamed at the horrors of my own imagination.

"Again?" Anne would ask.

"It's OK," I'd answer. "I'm OK. Go back to sleep."

"You have to talk to me about this."

"They're just dreams. There's nothing to talk about."

They were not just dreams. I could never see the stranger's face, but I always knew who it was. And no matter how many nights I tried, I still could not protect my brother.

◄ ►

I rarely caught Anne in a still pose. She was manic with energy, always painting or cleaning or reorganizing her collections of books and albums. One afternoon I returned to her room during a break between lectures to find her reading a book on the bed, lying there in a casual pose that I immediately knew was false. There was a table to the right of the door, and she had set a postcard on it, poking off the edge of the table so that it could not be missed.

"It came for you today. I didn't read it."

I believed her. She was nothing if not honest, but when she turned her attention back to her book, I knew she was also watching me as I read it. The postcard was from Etta. I don't know how she found me, and I don't know how many times I stood there and read it before Anne finally spoke.

"Is it from home?"

"I guess so."

"What does that mean? I guess so?"

"I guess it means that I'm not really sure where 'home' is."

"That's such bullshit, Warren. I let you off on so many things, but you have to give me something. I mean, really, what do I even know about you? You never talk to me."

"We talk all the time."

"You know what I mean. We don't talk about *you!*"

There was an uncertainty in Anne's expression that I had never seen in her before. She was waiting for something from me that we both knew I couldn't give her. I stuffed the postcard into my jacket, my whole history crumpled up in my pocket. Anne slammed her book shut and walked out. I had fooled myself for a time, but new lives can never supersede the old.

The dreams came when she came and left when she left, as if they existed solely to haunt my happiness. She told me she didn't think we should keep seeing each other, and I was both relieved and lost. It was the only time in my life that I had allowed myself to want something, but there was a freedom, still, in letting her go.

I continued to study my lessons and pass my courses, but it was an unfeeling repetition. I was completing my work with aptitude, but not passion. Halfway through my final semester, I finally realized that attending college wasn't my dream or my goal. Just like the meetings I'd stood through in Townsend's barn and the voter rally I'd gone to in Jackson, I was trying to live my brother's life.

Graden had never set foot outside of Mississippi. He knew that there was a world beyond it, but it existed for him only as a concept. He would never wade into an ocean, or look over the edge of a cliff, or see the colours of the northern lights flickering in the night sky. He would never feel mud between his toes that wasn't Mississippi mud, taste water that wasn't Mississippi water, breathe air that wasn't Mississippi air. I told him once that he would never leave the state. It made me cringe to think of it, one of many regrets I had. Instead of Graden, I was the one seeing the country, and he was the one left behind. I was the one getting an education, and he was the one who never graduated. I was the one who was still alive, and he was the one buried in a shallow grave in the Mississippi clay. Nothing in life or death is deserved.

I packed a handful of clothes into the same duffel bag I had left Mississippi with and walked away. On my bed at the hostel, I left the records I'd collected in a crate with a note addressed to Anne. I doubt she ever got it, but I never knew for sure, and I preferred it that way.

I returned to campus only once, and that was for graduation. I stayed well back from the crowd, sitting in the shade of a massive oak, and watched the young men and women crossing the stage in their purple robes, their names called out one by one. At one point, I watched a thin black boy accept his diploma and shake hands with the chancellor. As the chancellor's watch glinted in the sunlight, the boy seemed to grow taller and heavier. His nose broadened and his eyes came alive, his features becoming Graden's features. Graden raised one hand over his head, proudly displaying the rolled-up piece of paper, beaming, confident, radiant. I stood, tears running down my cheeks, and clapped.

15

AMBLAN, 2008

I STEPPED OUT OF the cab and into the cold. I'd been here eleven years, and I still wasn't used to it, although I had learned how to brace myself for it each time. Taking that first punch of frozen air into the lungs and holding it, swallowing the shock of it and allowing it to disperse throughout the body before exhaling, so that the second breath had no teeth.

I cinched the collar of my jacket as the cab pulled away, and I shuffled along the sidewalk to Martin's Market. The chimes above the door jingled as I entered. I removed my cap and nodded to the owner.

"Mornin', Todd."

"Mornin', Mr. Daniel."

"Just stocking up, case I get shut in later this week. You reckon this storm's gonna hit like they say?"

"Well, weather's pretty easy to predict this time of year. It's gonna snow, and it's gonna be cold. It's all just a matter of how much."

I smiled and picked up a grocery basket from the pile beside the door. I walked past the two aisles of hardware and cleaning products, past the breads and the slim selection of fresh fruit, and started stacking the basket with tins of stew, fish, and corn.

"See you got yourself a project going on up at your place," I said. "What ya workin' on over there, anyway?"

Todd called his answer out over the aisle. "Wife's got me building a sunroom. You believe that? A sunroom. Shit."

"Well, once a woman's got her mind set on something, there's no arguing with 'em."

"You're sure right there, Mr. Daniel."

Once the basket was half full, I loped to the checkout, struggling to lift it onto the counter. I emptied the contents then went back to fill it half full again. It was a small store and the selection was slim, but people here were loyal. In my third year here, a grocery chain opened a supermarket two streets over with wide, bright aisles stocked with every product anyone here could ever need, but few shoppers patronized it and within eight months the chain had closed up and moved out, leaving their brand new building behind. I placed the second load on the counter and rifled through my pockets to pay.

"That all? Hell, you gonna waste away to nothing."

"I wish you'd tell that to ole doc. He wants me to lose twenty more pounds. Says it'd be good for my knees. I told him I'd just as soon lose the knees as lose the weight."

Todd chuckled and packed the groceries into plastic bags.

"Well, if it gets rough in the next couple of days, I'll try and have one of the Hutches swing out and check on ya."

"Much obliged, but I reckon I'll be just fine. Been through a lot worse than some bad weather to get this old, a lot worse. And I figure to keep getting older for a while yet."

I winked and collected my groceries, listening to the chime as I pushed open the door and walked out into the street.

◀ ▶

At home, I unpacked the grocery bags and placed the tins of food in the cupboard. There was laughter from the other room, an old *Cheers* repeat. I had been collecting food for the past week, and was now satisfied with the stack of canned meats and noodles that I had amassed. My first winter here I had paid no mind to warnings about the ferocity of the storms that could hit and spent six days without power, curled beneath every blanket I had and eating nothing but crackers and dry cereal until Jared Hutchinson showed up. He stood in the doorway with an armful of groceries and a knowing grin.

"Welcome to Amblan." He walked into my kitchen like he owned it. I liked him right away.

He had parked his truck on the far side of the hill and hiked through the woods behind my house. He said it was easiest that way because my side of the hill faces the lake and gets far more deeply trenched in snow. He said places like mine are the ones the real estate agents always try to sell in the summer. He cut thick slabs of meat from a smoked ham and laughed without judgement when I told him what I'd paid. We ate sandwiches with cheese and pickles and drank beer from bottles slushed with ice in the necks. He left me with enough groceries to last a week or more, although the road was cleared after three more days.

I missed the intensity of the southern sun, some days so hot there was nothing to do but drink and sweat. I missed bread still warm from the oven and homemade macaroni and cheese and the greasy smear of pork rinds, but understanding how to prepare for them, I learned to love the winters here. The snow laid itself out thick and clean and sparkled brightly under the clear moon, the undersides of spruce and pine offering a rare hint of green. The air had a crisp quality and the cold imposed an honest harshness. Most of all, there was the quiet. There were no artificial sounds. A dog scratching through the frozen earth at the base of a tree. Curled and crippled leaves scuttling crablike across the newly fallen snow. The song of it, dry and haunting. A moose bellowing in the distance. And sometimes, no sound at all.

I mixed a can of soup with water from the kettle and sat down to watch television. I pulled a blanket across my waist and watched Sam and Henri compete for the phone numbers of a string of poofy-haired women. I ate the soup in big slurping spoonfuls, then set the bowl aside, and fell asleep in the chair, basking in the glow of the television set.

16

AMBLAN, 2008

I FIRST NOTICED HIM, sitting by himself at a corner table at Fryar's Grillhouse. His hat and boots looked newly bought, and I could tell from the sheen on the boots that he hadn't water-proofed them yet. His dark skin had blanched in the cold, turning his face an ashy grey. He kept his coat on while he looked at the menu, one hand holding it, one hand stuffed in his pocket. He put the menu down, checked how much money he had in his wallet, then looked at it again and made his choice. When the waitress arrived, he stiffened and sat further back in his chair, discreetly scanning the dining room. I looked away. Our eyes never met. He ordered a beef brisket with potatoes and peas, ate it in silence, paid his bill, and left.

I saw him again a few days later at the library, hunched over a microfiche reader, a pair of glasses set precariously on his nose, his head cocked forward at an odd angle so he could peer out of the bottom of the lenses. I approached the library desk.

"Morning, Mr. Daniel."

"Mornin', Barb."

"Your magazines are in."

"Good news. Looks like it's going to be reading weather for a while."

She pulled a stack of magazines from behind the desk.

"You know I don't mind getting these sent here, but I don't see why you don't just have these mailed to your house."

"Well then, what excuse would I have to come in and see you?" I smiled at her, then nodded towards the microfiche area. "Who's the new fella, Barb? Haven't seen him around before."

She looked around and seemed to notice the man for the first time.

"Don't know. He's come in a couple of times this week. Didn't catch a name. He just sits over there and reads old papers."

I made a point of walking past the microfiche reader on my way out the door, but I couldn't make out what he was looking at. The man didn't look at me as I passed.

I didn't see him again for almost a week. Near the beginning of church service, Reverend Scott asked if there were any new or visiting members who would like to introduce themselves. He looked directly to the back of the church as he did so, smiling warmly, and I turned to follow his gaze. The black man sat in the back pew, at the edge closest to the door, and although several others had also turned to face him, he sat stone-like, as if in doing so he wouldn't be seen. After an awkward moment, Reverend Scott cleared his throat and continued with the service, still smiling, though less genuinely. I looked back again later in the service, but the man was gone.

◄ ►

I was already on my way to join the Hutch brothers who were sitting at the window table in the coffee shop when I noticed him again, this time sitting in the corner, his back to the wall, scribbling left-handed in a notebook.

"Earl."

Jared Hutchinson had spotted me and was waving me over. The man in the corner looked up when Jared called my name and tucked the pad and pen away in a knapsack he had on the chair beside him.

I sat at the table with Jared and his older brother, Barry. Both stank of sweat and whiskey, which meant a day of ice-fishing. The waitress freshened up both their cups, then looked at me and hesitated. "I thought the doc said you wasn't supposed to have caffeine, Mr. Daniel."

I turned the cup in front of me over, indicating that she fill it.

"I done outlived every doctor I ever had, and if this one's the doctor that finally sees me into the ground, it'll be with a stomach full of coffee and a liver full of rye."

She filled the cup as the Hutch brothers laughed heartily, and I winked at her as she walked away. She stopped at the table in the corner, but the man covered his cup with his hand and declined a refill. I turned my attention back to the Hutches.

"Catch anything today?"

"Nothing worth keeping." Barry snorted. "Sat in that damn lodge all morning and didn't haul up nothing hardly big enough to swallow the bait."

Jared shook his head. "Probably don't help when you piss down the damn hole."

"Well, hell, I ain't going out to whip out my pecker in the cold. I'm liable to piss right through that ice and have it break underneath me."

"Well, pissing in that hut, you're likely to have some dumb fish mistake that little thing for a worm and jump right out the hole for a nibble."

"Shit."

Barry elbowed his brother playfully and looked at me. I glanced over my shoulder at the man in the corner, who in turn was staring out the window.

"Friend o' yours, Earl?"

I looked back, shook my head. "Just noticed him around, that's all."

Jared turned to the corner, then turned back. "Yeah, I seen him here and there, showed up about a week ago, I think. He's staying at the McLarens' old place."

"Know who he is?"

Jared shrugged, grabbed the sides of his chair, and hopped twice out away from the table, so that he was half-facing me and half-facing the other man.

"Hey, there. Name's Jared, this here is my brother Barry, and this is Earl."

The man looked at Jared warily, like an animal backed against a wall. He nodded, and Jared continued.

"New to these parts?"

"Yes, sir."

Jared pushed his brother on the shoulder. "Sir. Did you hear that? Sir. Now that's respect." Both brothers chuckled, and Jared called back to the man in the corner, "Where you from?"

"Philadelphia."

The man sipped his coffee, never taking his eyes off Jared. I thought I detected a southern accent, but it was faint if it was there at all.

"Whoo, that's a long ways. What brings you all the way up here?"

The man hesitated for a moment before answering. "Hunting trip."

"Good huntin' up here," Barry chipped in. "I had a couple tourists in last year, took 'em up to a spot I know. They bagged a bull moose the size of a small elephant. I grabbed one edge of his antlers and couldn't reach the other edge. You looking for a good place to stake out, you just let me know."

"I appreciate the offer, but I'd just as soon stay on my own."

Jared shrugged. "Suit yourself. Some of these woods can be a little tricky though. And, not meaning to offend a fella, but truth be told, you don't look like a woodsman to me."

The man took another sip of coffee, then swirled the cup around once, looking at what remained. I thought that he looked at me, just once, and only briefly, before he put the cup down and answered.

"No offence taken. But some of us may be more than what we appear."

He dropped some change on the table, picked up his knapsack, and walked out the door.

17

AMBLAN, 2008

I DIDN'T SEE HIM AGAIN for a couple of days. I'd come back to town on Friday to grab a few final items, figuring that I was ready to hunker down for a bit. If the storm kept me locked in for any length of time, I had my magazines and food and gas for the generator so I was ready. The cab stopped at the crest of the hill, and the driver said he wouldn't go any further, despite the chains that he had illegally wrapped around his tires. It was one of the rare times that I wished I were still driving, but I hadn't had a licence since I'd come to Ontario.

I paid him and walked the rest of the way. The wind was down, but an occasional gust still whipped biting blasts across my cheeks. There were tire tracks, already mostly filled in, but they still gave me a somewhat shallower trench to hike through, and given the conditions, I had no concerns about walking down the middle of the road. It was a quiet road at the best of times, just an occasional hunter driving into the bush, but when it stormed, it was all but abandoned.

The snow was falling thick and heavy, and by the time I had walked a hundred yards the tracks were completely filled in. My legs ached. It was not much farther, and I was eager to get home, but I was careful to move slowly. I knew that moisture, not cold, was the danger, and I didn't want to perspire.

When I got to the front step, I struggled to pull the outer screen door open against the wind. My fingers were stiff, and I was grateful that I didn't have to pry them around a key. Not locking my door was one of the most difficult adjustments I'd made when I moved here. It seemed naïve to leave the door unlocked, but after I came to understand the remoteness of the house, the space between neighbours, and the familiarity of everyone in the town, it eventually seemed more foolish to lock the door than not.

The mat inside the front hall was already wet with melted snow.

"Hello?" I called out.

The foyer was just a small square meant to brace the rest of the house from the cold of opening doors and, as such, didn't offer a view into the other rooms. I hung my coat on its peg, slipped off my boots, then pulled off my wet socks as well.

I walked slowly into the kitchen. Nothing seemed out of place.

"Hutch?"

The house echoed silence, an accusation of foolishness aimed at an old man. The mat had probably just not dried from when I left in the morning. I poured myself a glass of water from the tap and went to sit in the living room. I flicked on the television, but most channels were either wavering columns of black and white or completely obliterated with buzzing static. I knew that turning the antenna wasn't likely to produce results any more favourable.

It was when I stood up to select a DVD from the shelf that I noticed the empty rack above the fireplace where my rifle should have been hung. I heard footsteps on the stairs.

The black man appeared in the archway, his face stony. He still wore his coat, and his boots leaked dirty water onto the hardwood floor. He was hunched into his shoulders as if he was unable to shake off the cold, and his short grey hair still shone with gathered snow. His expression was difficult to read, but he had the look of a hard man, of someone who had suffered and

survived. Hutch was right, he didn't look like much of a woodsman, but I had no doubt that he knew how to use a rifle and that
he was willing to do so. I'd seen him in the restaurant, seeming to
struggle with his right hand, but he held the rifle steady, and he
looked sure of himself. His stare didn't waver as he lifted it and
pointed it at me.

I raised my hands and waited, sure of what he would ask
before he spoke. His mouth opened onto the past. His lips were
white and cracked, and a name eleven years dead formed in the
space between them.

"Are you Earl Olsen?"

There was no need to answer. I left the DVD on the shelf
and sat.

18

NEW YORK, 1962

I TOOK MY FATHER'S first name as my last. Daniel Olsen was born in 1919 in New York City. My grandparents tried five times to have children, but only two survived birth — my father, Daniel, and my uncle, Patrick. From what I was told, they grew up in relative comfort, but like most families they lost almost everything during the Depression. My father dropped out of school at sixteen and lied about his age to get a job in a foundry. He worked fourteen-hour days, smelting iron for a fraction of the pay that the other workers were getting.

My father went to a local soup kitchen each afternoon, the only meal that he allowed himself. It was there that he met my mother. They married quickly and were youthfully happy for a couple of years, but the Depression was worsening. Shortly after I was born, my father lost his job and couldn't find another one. He spent his days scavenging for scrap metal to sell, or for any stray items that might be useful. He would come home carrying assorted pieces of junk that my mother would then scrub clean and try to spin into treasures. She painted rusty tin jars and set them out as colour-ful planters, polished sections of old cast-iron fencing and hooked them together to make elaborate ornament shelves, even hung a section of branch from the dining-room ceiling and wrapped it with white Christmas lights to serve as a rustic chandelier.

She tried to work the same miracle with my clothes. They were sewn together from scraps, and cardboard filled the holes in my shoes. My father sometimes brought home a few stalks of wilted flowers that he'd found or picked somewhere. Mother would coo over them and place them in an empty pop can filled with water for display, mostly to salvage my father's pride. Despite the hardships I learned of later, there were seldom arguments.

I have clear memories of baseball. Every weekend the kids from the neighbourhood would mill around in the streets, waiting for enough people to show up or for someone to find a piece of wood that was sturdy enough to be used for a bat. We would play until dark and afterwards, when most of the kids had left, my father would return home. He would stay outside with me for another hour, just throwing the ball back and forth under the flickering streetlights. I would always greet him the same way.

"Find anything good today?"

He would shrug. "A few things. We'll see what your mother can do with them."

"I could help. I could go with you."

I offered every time, and every time he would just smile and toss the ball back to me.

My favourite moments came when my father was able to find books. We would gather at night by the light of candles wedged into the tops of old pop bottles, and he'd read to me from the stained and yellowing pages. Sometimes there were pages missing, and Dad would fill in the story as best he could, either from memory or imagination.

There were rarely visitors. Uncle Patrick is the only one I recall, and although times must have been as hard for him as for us, he never showed it. Whenever he arrived, his shoes were shined and his shirt was gleaming white. His face was flushed, as if he ran over to our house each time to visit. He was loud and charming and full of plans. I secretly wished my father were more like him.

It was Uncle Patrick who went south first. He convinced my father that manufacturing and industry were dying and that the only chance a man had was agriculture. He was working on a deal to secure a piece of property in Mississippi and wanted us to move down there with him. It led to one of the rare arguments in our household. I lay in the bed at night, listening to snatches.

"We're getting by, Daniel. Things aren't great, but we're getting by."

"Getting by? We're not getting by. Almost everything we own is made out of garbage. There's no work, and there ain't likely to be any for a while. Patrick can get us a piece of land."

"Your brother is always chasing some scheme, Daniel. You told me so yourself. Are you going to put our future in his hands? Earl's future?"

"Oh, don't throw that at me! You know I want what's best for Earl just as much as you do. But what future does he have here?"

"Whatever future we make for him."

My mother and father continued whispering their disagreement to one another, voices occasionally rising to the point that I could make them out, then dropping again.

I never heard another word about it after that night, but I could tell by the sudden hush whenever I entered the room that the discussion continued for several weeks, and I could tell by the look on their faces who was winning. Uncle Patrick visited us a final time in our tiny house in Queens. Father clapped him on the back and assured him that we would be on our way to join him soon. My mother smiled faintly, but offered no objection, and it seemed the issue was settled.

Shortly after that, my mother's coughing began.

◄ ►

In hindsight my mother went quickly, but it didn't seem that way at the time. She tried to hide her symptoms at first. I would see her stop and tremble occasionally while she was scrubbing our clothes or peeling potatoes for dinner, and I knew that she was fighting to contain the raw hacking with which she began each day. She had an old kerchief that she used, and I tracked her descent by the colour of the cloth — at first speckled with red spots, then stained a dark maroon, then black.

She spent shorter and shorter periods on her feet, and within a couple of weeks, she was bedridden. She became a shape beneath the sheets, a flash of golden hair splayed across the pillowcase, the hair growing thinner and paler as she grew smaller, as if the bed were slowly absorbing her into itself.

The house grew dingy and grey. Tufts of dust collected on the baseboards. The sculptures and trinkets that she had cleaned and crafted turned back into garbage, rusty and old. My mother had transformed our home through sheer force of will, but as her will faded, the house and everything in it reverted to its natural state. My father started sleeping in the living room. He stopped lighting candles at night.

I woke one morning in early April, the air still cold and dry, the sun strong enough to gleam through the curtains. There was no coughing. The door to my mother's bedroom was closed. There was nothing my father needed to say.

My father and I spent a full day scrubbing the house. We hosted a small service and sent everyone home too quickly. My father was too proud to let everyone know we couldn't afford a burial. My mother was interred in the paupers' section of the graveyard with no headstone and no marker. My father spent the next month in a fugue-like state, barely functional. When he emerged, we began to pack for Mississippi.

19

AMBLAN, 2008

THE MAN SITTING across from me looked different than he did on television. In the interviews, his eyes had looked like they were rimmed in shadows, his cheeks sunken and thin. Sitting across from me now, he appeared stronger and more vigorous than I remembered: his face was round, the cheeks almost plump, though sagging. The sockets of his eyes were dragged down as well, showing a thin line of red above the lower lids. It gave his face the impression of being intently alert. His skin was grey from the cold, and he looked bulky, still bundled up in his coat.

His left hand rested loosely on the rifle, and his right hand was hidden in his pocket. The boots continued to leak dirty water on to the living room floor. I asked him to remove them, and for a second he blinked and looked confused.

"Your boots," I said. "They're wet. I'd appreciate it if you would remove them."

He ignored the request and shifted the rifle on his lap.

"I'm guessing you know who I am," he said. His words came out in a slow, deep rattle, the sound of a man who didn't have to raise his voice to be heard.

"I've seen you on television. Newspapers too. News this far north doesn't care much about stuff down in the States."

"Well, you must have gone to some trouble to get it then."

"And you must have gone to some trouble to get here."

We stared at each other for a moment.

"You look awful cold. I could fix you some tea. I'm guessing from the looks of you that we'll be here awhile."

I rolled out of the chair and ambled past him into the kitchen, not waiting for a reply. I listened for sounds of movement while I boiled the water and poured two cups, but didn't hear a thing and when I walked back into the room with the tea, it looked as if he hadn't moved. I handed him the cup, and he took it carefully in both hands. I could see why he had kept the right one hidden — the outside two fingers were clipped and what remained had atrophied. The other two fingers were hooked as well, though less so, and there were dark scars raised along the skin on the back of his hand and down onto his wrist. He blew the steam from his cup and, catching me looking, twisted his right hand towards me in a mock wave.

"I got this for touching a white girl."

I didn't know how to respond. To say it had nothing to do with me would likely make him angry, to offer an apology would probably make him more so. He was clearly on edge, and I felt like any mistake might set him off. When he dropped his hand he rested the fingers on the trigger guard.

"I'll answer your question," I said. "I am Earl Olsen. I'm sure that comes as no surprise to you."

"No surprise. Bit surprised to hear you own up to it, though. You know, a lot of folks seem to think you're dead."

"Well, they probably ain't far off with their guess."

"And you been hiding up here, all this time."

"I told you. Folks up here don't care much about all of that."

"But you've been keeping an eye out."

I sipped my tea and forced myself to remain calm while I tried figure out what he wanted. If it was just revenge, he could have shot me clean already. If he wanted to bring me to justice, maybe he was secretly taping our conversation and planned on turning me over to the FBI. If so, he already had my name and that was about all he needed. That didn't seem to be his motive, though. In pursuing the others involved in the case, he had always leaned on police and news investigators to do the work. He was just the name applying pressure, the face showing up at the end of the trail to shine a spotlight on the case. The fact that he had come here by himself meant that this was something different. I couldn't find any way to spin that fact that didn't mean trouble for me, but I wasn't just going to sit meekly by and be threatened in my own house.

"I suppose you've suffered quite a bit over the years," I said. "I'm not gonna pretend that's not true. You're not the only one, though. You're right. I've been keeping an eye out."

"Not the only one? Not the only one who has suffered?"

He leaned forward and snorted with disgust. His eyes narrowed and his lips curled, baring his teeth, but his expression quickly settled back to its look of bland focus. His was an old anger, flashing across his face but not holding, like an engine that wouldn't quite turn over. It was an anger he had lived with for decades and vented many times. My own anger was fresher and had never before found voice.

"My daddy didn't deserve to die in no prison." I spit the words at him, but he didn't flinch. "Yeah, I been keeping an eye on the case all right. And I was *excited* when I first found out about it. My daddy never wanted any part of what happened to your brother. Hell, I tried to find you when I heard the case was reopening. By the time I found how to get ahold of you, you already had my daddy square in your crosshairs."

I had watched in disbelief as my father was the first one to be dragged out his front door in handcuffs, the lone strand of white hair on his head, flopping in the wind. He could barely walk under his own power, and yet they had his arms behind his back and were herding him into the police car like some danger-ous criminal, reporters throwing questions and accusations at him while he looked around in bewilderment.

The others followed, one by one, and though I had no sym-pathy for any of them, I grew to hate Warren more and more each time I saw that sunken look. He was the perpetual inno-cent, the perpetual victim. As I stared across at him now, I'm sure that hatred was naked on my face.

"I couldn't even see him at the end, you know that? My daddy. I tried to go see him, but he wouldn't let me. Knew that I couldn't show up there without letting the authorities know who I really was. My daddy died in prison all alone. Died with just a chaplain and the warden by his bedside, damn near strangers."

The man listened with no change in expression, but his voice quivered with a barely held rage. "It's more than what my brother had. Your father got what he deserved."

"And you saw to that didn't you? You saw that he got what he deserved. You don't know nothing about my father. You don't know what he *deserved*."

"I know what he did."

"What he did. What happened to that brother of yours was terrible, I know that. And I won't deny my own guilt, but my father was a good man."

"Did your daddy ever seen this? What about you?"

He reached inside his jacket and pulled out a faded black-and-white photo. It was his brother laid out on a table in the coroner's office, bones broken, flesh on his chest torn nearly in strips, eyes mostly rotted so that there were just two balls of gel-atin in the sockets.

He said, "The scales of justice don't work the way you think they do. They're not balanced. You do one terrible thing, it doesn't wipe out one good thing you done. It wipes out every good thing you done. So go ahead. Go on and tell me about this peach of a daddy of yours."

I had not seen the photo before. It brought me back to that room. The plink of water dripping from an unsealed joist. The smell of damp wood mixing with the stench of the boy's sweat and shit and piss. The bloodied shirt balled up in the corner, and the rough feel of the rusty pliers in my hand.

There was another photo as well, the corner of it poking out from beneath the first. They must have stuck together inside Warren's jacket. I slowly reached across the table to separate them.

The second photo was taken on the steps of the courthouse in Jackson. They were all there — Marty Bavon with his cauliflower ears and an evil, yellow-toothed grin; Blaine Pimpton, smirking at the crowd as if sharing a joke; Rob and Barry Tywater jabbing each other with elbows like school kids; Paul Poust staring straight into the camera with a crooked smile; Uncle Patrick leading the group down the steps, suit jacket open, hands in pockets, and wearing the smug look of a man who believes himself vindicated. My father walked with his head down and I was beside him, wide-eyed and bewildered. God, I was so young. But so was the boy on the coroner's table.

I looked back and forth between the two photos. With the exception of my father, I hated every one of the men in the courthouse photo, even Uncle Patrick, and I hated myself for ever having respected them, for having wanted so badly to be one of them.

I couldn't stomach what they'd done to that boy, and I hadn't seen what ended up of him before now. The last time I saw him, I had turned away and let my father do what I could not.

20

MISSISSIPPI, 1964

THE TRIP FROM NEW YORK to Mississippi was a blur. Everything we owned fit into two suitcases that were loaded into the trunk of the bus. We sat mostly in silence. The buildings changed from tall to short, from packed tightly together to dotted across wide expanses, from grey metal and glass to wood and shingle. The highway turned from asphalt to dusty country roads, and the rise in temperature was palpable as we rode farther and farther into the south. It was my first look at the rest of America.

There were a few stops along the way, allowing the travellers to stretch their legs or get some lunch. We took hurried bathroom breaks in turns, my father concerned that if we both left the bus, we might lose our seats and not be allowed back on. Mostly we stayed on the bus, sharing a ham sandwich on stale bread and an apple, both of which he had tucked protectively inside his jacket.

When we finally arrived, we stepped off the bus and were immediately assaulted by dirt and heat. Dust clung to the frayed hems of my pants and to the stitches holding my shoes together. I felt my father's hand sweating against my own as we waited for the driver to unload the bags. The man in front of us tipped the driver a quarter when he received his bags. My father let go of my hand and walked away to avoid the embarrassment of not being able to do the same. The driver pulled our cases off the pile, frowned at me, then set the bags onto the ground. I dragged them across the dirt lot, and when I reached my father in the shade of the station's porch, I was drenched in sweat.

My father looked more tired than I had ever seen him. He gave me a thin smile and started to say something, but was interrupted by a blast from a car horn. We both turned. Uncle Patrick was seated behind the steering wheel of a blue Ford truck, waving cheerily out the window. He fumbled with the door, then got out and brushed himself off with his hat. His clean white shirt and crisp tan pants and the burst of colour in his cheeks were in utter contrast to my father's shabby, dirty clothes and the ghostly pallor of his face.

If Uncle Patrick took any notice of our appearance, he didn't show it. He flapped his hat and smiled broadly at us. "Welcome to Mississippi."

◄ ►

In Mississippi, I learned that I was poor. Back in New York, the other teens I knew were no better off than I was, and so it had never occurred to me how badly off we really were. I'd overheard people talking at store counters and on porches about how tough times were, the words coming thick and slow through the southern drawl, but to my eyes that wasn't the case.

Still, I noticed that the other kids here wore clean, pressed clothes that were generally in good condition, their hair parted neatly or sometimes slicked back. They rode shiny new bicycles. The older kids were occasionally allowed to drive their father's truck or car, and their houses, while not always large, were well kept and set on swaths of open land.

It was the space that I had the most trouble getting used to. In the city we could almost always hear our neighbours, but in

Mississippi I could shine a flashlight at night and not see another house, other than my uncle's.

Uncle Patrick had asked us to stay with him, but my father's pride would not allow it. Instead we stayed in a tiny clapboard house at the back of his property, a converted servants' quarters. Uncle Patrick had bought a small patch of land and had been successful enough growing peanuts on it that he had been able to purchase some of the adjoining fields as well. My father worked each day in my uncle's fields, and although I offered to help, he was insistent that I stay in school. Other than suppers together in the main house, the fees for my education were the only charity my father accepted from my uncle.

I started my junior year of high school in the fall, but it was a struggle. I had no real interest in my studies. I was ashamed of the patchwork clothing I wore, and the dirt that I could never quite get out from under my fingernails. I was mistrusted by most of the other kids because I had come from the north. Three of the senior boys snickered at me as I walked past one day, and I heard one of them say that my father and I "lived like coons." I broke his nose with one clean shot, before his friends wrestled me to the ground and started kicking me.

My father talked to me about turning the other cheek and trying harder to fit in, while my uncle watched with a dark expression on his face and said nothing. That night they argued. I crept to the edge of the house and crouched beneath a window to listen.

" ... things are different down here, Daniel. Trying to make it on your own just ain't the way to go. Not for you or the boy."

"I've already told you, Patrick. I don't want no part of that. I appreciate everything you've done to help us, but I will pay back everything we owe and more, once I get my feet settled."

"Shit. Get your feet settled? What are you hoping for? That you can scrape out some kind of living on your own, keep your head just above the surface, always one day away from losing it all? Is that what you want?"

"I'm just not fond of taking charity, that's all. Particularly from the kind of people you're talking about. I know about the meetings you go to. I know the kind of people that are getting in and out of those shiny cars that show up in the driveway every week."

"Now you hold on just a minute! Those are fine people. Look around you. I'm doing good here, Daniel. That doesn't come without a cost. These people that you're turning your nose up at have helped me. They've protected me. And they can do the same for you."

"I don't think I need protection, Patrick."

"And what about your boy? You got him living in a damn shack, coming home from school with a black eye and a bloody lip. You don't think he could use a little protection?"

"The kids that did that ain't got nothing to do with ..."

"The kids that did that do what they're told. If they're told to stay away from someone, they stay away. Everyone here does what they're told, Daniel. That's how things work here, and you'll learn that one way or the other. I sure as shit hope it's the easy way."

I crawled back to the shack and laid down on the cot. I had seen the difference in how people looked at my father and how people looked at my uncle. I assumed it was just a familiarity that my uncle had built up in the years that he had been here, but now I knew that it was more. I stared up at the ceiling and dreamed of the men my uncle spoke of. I dreamed of being accepted, of being respected. Maybe even of being feared. I had no idea who my father and uncle had argued about, but I knew that I wanted to be one of them.

◄ ►

I started to steal things. They were minor items at first, mostly candy or soda or sometimes a piece of fruit. I was sure that the storekeeper, Greely, caught me one time. He looked up from the counter just after I had slipped a bar of soap into my pocket, but he merely held my gaze for a moment, then went back to reading his paper. Sweating, I turned and walked out the door. I bathed that night with fresh soap, and I had never felt cleaner.

I grew bolder as I grew more successful. I stole a bicycle from the backyard of one of the senior boys who had beaten me. I stole three watermelons off the back of a cart bound for the market. I cracked one of them open around the back of a horse stall and devoured it hurriedly in the heat of the midday sun, then walked home with the other two under my arm as if I had just bought them, nodding and smiling at everyone I passed on the way. I stole a baseball glove, knowing that I could never show it to my father, never use it to play catch with him.

Most of the items I stole were out in the open and only required the nerve to pick them up. Only once did I break in to a place to steal something.

Tom Woodson was the local tailor, a frail wisp of a man who looked much older than his years. One afternoon, when the streets were quiet, I skipped class and slipped into the back of his store from the laneway, climbing through a window that had been propped open for air. I listened carefully to the noises outside while I tried on shoes in the near-dark of the storeroom. Several times I heard Mr. Woodson walk past the door, but he never stopped. After what seemed like an impossibly long time, I found a pair of shoes that fit me. I tucked them under my jacket, climbed out the same way I had come in, and sprinted almost the whole way home.

The next day I dressed as I normally did, in a faded but neatly pressed shirt and pants worn thread-thin in some parts. I tied the laces on my regular stitched-together shoes and presented myself at breakfast. My father doled a spoonful of grits onto my plate.

"Are you having any, Pop?"

My father gave me a thin smile, then walked out the door for a day in the fields.

. I waited until I finished my grits, then went back into my room to change my shoes. I told myself that I didn't care what the other kids at school thought, but I knew it wasn't true. I wanted them to look past my shabby clothes and notice my new shoes instead. I wanted them to ignore my northern accent and the servants' quarters where we lived, and — although I was ashamed to admit it — to forget my dad and his stubborn insistence on doing things his way.

When I arrived at school, the shoes drew more attention than I had intended.

◀ ▶

My father was waiting for me when I got home. One of the teachers had taken it upon himself to drive all the way out to our home to tell my father about my new shoes and to politely imply that they could not possibly be mine.

My father marched me barefoot back into town, shoes in hand. Mr. Woodson was idly wiping the counter in his shop when we walked in. He looked at me, looked at the shoes, looked at my father, then went right back to his cleaning. My father nudged me forward. I cleared my throat, but when I spoke, I still could hear a nervous squeak in my voice.

"Mr. Woodson." He looked up from his cleaning, and I held up the shoes. "Mr. Woodson, sir. I have come here to make an apology to you."

Woodson's hollow cheeks captured the shadows in the room, making it seem like his eyes were flat grey lights just floating in darkness. There was no expression on his face. I could feel my father's heated stare behind me. I continued.

"Mr. Woodson, I stole these shoes from your storeroom. They do not belong to me. I would like to return them, sir, and to say I'm sorry."

"Well, that's all right there, Earl. Boys will be boys, I guess."

I was stunned. I had expected him to be angry. I stepped forward to put the shoes on his counter, but he raised his hand to stop me.

"Keep them."

There was a moment of silence. I turned to look at my father, who came to stand beside me.

"I appreciate your patience, Mr. Woodson, but that is not an option."

Woodson put down his cloth and leaned over the counter, his lean face now coming fully into the light. He ignored my father and looked at me.

"Your uncle came to see me earlier. Those are your shoes now, son."

My father looked as if he'd been punched in the stomach. He took a deep breath. I could almost see the anger welling up in him, first his hands closing, then his shoulders tightening, and his jaw clenching. When he spoke, I could tell it was an effort for him to keep his voice calm.

"My brother is a generous man," my father said, "but my son has not earned these shoes, and he is here to give them back."

"Well, Mr. Olsen, your brother made it clear to me that the boy is to have them shoes, so I'm afraid I have to disregard your wishes. I can't take 'em back."

I stood holding the shoes while they stared at each other. My father was a proud man, but this was not his world. It was apparent even to me that things worked differently here than they did back in New York, in ways that neither of us could quite understand. What I did understand was that my uncle knew this place and had made it work for him. And I also knew that my father never would.

He grabbed my arm and spun me towards the door. I could feel him burning with shame the entire walk home, and I regretted having brought us to this.

We reached Uncle Patrick's house just in time to see a polished black Studebaker leaving the driveway. Uncle Patrick sat on the porch, smoking a cigar. We started towards our quarters in the back, but my father jerked my arm to force me to stop. He looked at the shoes in my hand, then at my feet, dirty and blistered, and bleeding slightly from the walk. He turned to the porch without a word, and I followed.

He stood in front of Uncle Patrick, but couldn't look him in the eye. Uncle Patrick exhaled a thick mouthful of smoke. He had won and my father had lost, though at what I wasn't yet sure. My uncle crushed out his cigar.

"There is something come up we could use some help with."

My father nodded at Uncle Patrick, then turned to me.

"Go back to the house," he said. "Your uncle and I have some things to talk about."

I was frightened, but I knew that whatever was about to happen was because of me. I could still see the Studebaker driving away, glistening in the late afternoon sun. I looked at my father, with his head hung, and I couldn't picture him ever being a man in one of those cars, couldn't picture him as one of the men that commanded the respect that my uncle clearly held.

I had never openly defied my father before, but I stepped up onto the porch beside my uncle, my new shoes in hand.

"I'm staying. If there's something you need help with, I can help too."

21

AMBLAN, 2008

I HAD NEVER TOLD my father's story before. When I moved here, I hadn't just changed my name; I'd tried to make a completely fresh start. I deliberately broke off contact with everyone from my past, other than my father. I drove across the border with a Mississippi licence, then cut it to pieces once I arrived. I burned every photo except one, a faded shot of my parents holding hands shortly after their wedding. I paid cash for the little winterized cottage on the hill, avoiding any official paperwork, collected my magazines at the library to avoid having anything sent to the house, and had the post office hold my mail for a weekly pickup for the same reason.

It was only by chance that I had caught word of Warren's efforts to reopen the investigation. Jared Hutchinson was guiding a couple of hunters from northern Michigan, in town for buck season. They had seen a piece on television about it and mentioned it while they were out on the trail. Jared repeated the story while we sat in the coffee shop later in the day, incredulous that someone could still be tried for something that they'd done some forty-odd years earlier. I excused myself clumsily and spent the next few days holed up in the cottage before deciding to use the library computers to find out whatever I could.

Now, Warren Williams was sitting in my living room. It was hard to recall all of the details of that former life, the crushing poverty, the sudden move south, the struggle not just to survive but to somehow fit in.

"My daddy did a terrible thing, I know that. He got involved in something horrendous, but it was my fault he got involved. He wasn't one of those folks. He shouldn't have his name up beside theirs."

"I got no interest in assigning fault."

"That a fact? You sure do seem to have put a lot of time and effort into finding out a whole lot about all of us. If you're not interested in hearing about it now, then what are you doing here? And how did you find me?"

He shifted in his seat, seeming to favour his left leg.

"Someone saw your face on the news. Called and told me you were here. Wasn't anything difficult."

"And you came all this way to see for yourself."

"Everybody that had a hand in my brother's killing is either passed on or behind bars. Only one living free is you."

"You make it sound so damn simple, and it wasn't like that at all. There was a lot of things going on back then, it was complicated. You, the courts, the FBI, the media. You ever think that maybe, just maybe, you don't know what really went on that night?"

Warren was growing agitated. The anger that had flashed briefly returned, and this time it held. He uncrossed his legs and leaned forward, gripping his hands tighter on the rifle.

"I know plenty about what happened that night. I know that he was beat for hours. I know that his chest was carved up. I know he was castrated. I know he lived through it all and was still alive when he was dumped in the swamp. I know more about that night than I would ever want to know in a hundred lifetimes."

"So you're gonna set things straight then? You're gonna ... haul me in and make everything right with the world. What do you really think you've accomplished so far? I'll tell you what. Nothing! Nothing's changed, and sending me off to prison ain't gonna change nothing either."

He pulled himself up to his feet. "I don't need to change things. Never did. But you think you somehow got the right to walk around free just because *time* has passed? You don't."

"Well, where's the police then? That's how you work, ain't it? Showing up on the front lawn of doddering old men with half the police squad and three different news teams. You're a regular celebrity. Just about that time, isn't it? Call 'em in! Hope you got all cleaned up for the camera."

It seemed I had hit a nerve, because Warren was angrily clenching and unclenching his jaw. "Don't need news teams for this. Don't need police neither."

"And what makes me so special?"

"You're the one who knows what I want to know."

"What's that?"

His voice shook as he spoke, although whether it was fury or grief I couldn't tell. There was a shift of mood in the room, and I was suddenly licking my lips, more nervous than I cared to admit.

"I want to know why didn't you take me too?"

22

MISSISSIPPI, 1964

UNCLE PATRICK BOUGHT ME a new pair of woollen pants and a crisp white shirt. They were the nicest clothes I had ever worn. They would have matched perfectly with the shoes I had stolen from Woodson's storeroom, but I refused to wear them, choosing my old, worn and patched shoes instead. My father looked at the shoes, but said nothing.

He eyed me nervously. "This is a man's work, son."

"I'm ready for it, sir."

"I hope that's not true. This ain't the kind of thing a man should ever be ready for. You don't need to do this."

"This is what's best."

"It ain't up to you to decide what's best. I'm still your father."

"And I appreciate everything you've done for me, but what's it gotten us? Either of us? I ain't never had anything nice my whole life. Mom's dead and buried in a hole someplace where I couldn't even find her if I tried. I don't blame you, I know you did the best you could, but don't you ever get tired of doing everything the hard way?"

My father turned away, staring out the door. He covered his eyes with hands as if he were upset at my words, but all he said was, "Son, every way is the hard way."

He walked out into the night, and I followed.

Gnats clustered in balls around the lamppost by the porch. There were six men gathered in my uncle's front yard, and three black cars in the driveway. The men were all similarly dressed and stood in a circle, smoking cigarettes. Uncle Patrick introduced us. There were firm handshakes, but few smiles.

"Breaking one in tonight, are we?"

The men laughed, and my face burned in embarrassment.

"He'll do fine." My uncle said. "Don't you worry about him. The kid's made of gritty stuff. Like his uncle. Like his pop."

Uncle Patrick looked at my dad as if waiting for confirmation.

"You think he's gonna be up there tonight?" one of the other men asked.

"Up there once a week, at least. Sometimes more. I'd lay pretty good odds on it."

"Well, if he is, then I guess he ain't going to be rallying and stirring up trouble for much longer. We ready?"

The men stubbed out their cigarettes and started towards the cars. I filed alongside my father.

"Earl, why don't you get in with me."

My uncle gestured towards a car that he was entering. A mean-looking fellow with stubby ears and narrow teeth stood by the driver's side. My father placed his hand on my shoulder. I inhaled deeply, then shrugged his hand off and walked towards my uncle.

◄ ►

I remember the sound of gravel crunching under the tires and country music on the radio. In the darkness, the trees seemed closer to the road, as if they had inched forward at nightfall. My uncle and the stubby-eared man were in the front seat, talking and smoking. The car slowed. I leaned forward from where I was sitting in the back and saw a figure standing by the side of the road. When the headlights hit him, he turned.

"Is that him?" my uncle asked.

"Well," the other man said, "it's somebody."

He turned off the engine, and the night was suddenly loud with crickets. The three of us got out.

"Stay by the car," Uncle Patrick told me.

Stepping into the headlights, the stubby-eared man looked pale to the point of translucence, the effect enhanced by the glistening of sweat on his cheekbones and brow. His teeth, angled inward and stained yellow by cigarettes, gave him a goblin-like appearance in the glow. The boy who was standing at the side of the road was about my age, but much taller. He dipped his head slightly, but otherwise remained still while my uncle and the other man approached.

"How ya doin', son?"

"I'm good, sir."

"What are you doing out here this time of night?"

"Walking, sir."

"Walking." The stubby-eared man smiled at my uncle, but my uncle stayed silent.

"Don't look like you was walking. Look like you was just standing there."

"I was just resting for a minute, sir."

I watched the boy closely. He was careful to give nothing away, but it was clearly an effort for him. He clenched his fists once, then quickly released them.

"Well, it's awful late," the stubby-eared man continued. "Where you walking to this time of night?"

"Off to fetch my brother, sir."

"And where's your brother at?"

"Just up the road, sir. With some friends."

The boy started to fidget. He looked like he could knock us all down with just a few blows, but he was the one who was uneasy. I realized that I felt a little sorry for him. I didn't really know what he had done, other than Uncle Patrick's vague accusations of "stirring up trouble."

I had a sudden knot in my stomach. I hadn't pictured it like this. I had expected a wild, yelling Negro instigator, not this scared, quiet boy. I got up off the hood of the car and walked a few steps. I thought I saw something in the bushes. I strained my eyes, but the men were focussed on the boy. My uncle spoke for the first time.

"Do I know you, boy?"

"I don't know, sir."

"What's your name?

"Graden, sir."

"Graden. You're James Williams's boy, from off the other side of the woods."

"Yes, sir."

The boy's fear was apparent now, he was no longer trying to hide it or else no longer able to. He had to know now that we had come looking for him specifically. They toyed with him anyway, and the knot in my stomach grew as I watched it. I told myself that it would all be over soon, to just hold it together and do what I needed to. It was too late back out.

"You know this boy, huh?" said the stubby-eared man with a smirk.

"Hell, yes I do," my uncle replied. He spit on the dirt and spread his hands wide. "Just about everyone does. This here is the famous Graden Williams."

"Famous, huh? Famous on account of what?"

"Well, he famous 'cause he's almost white." My uncle laughed. "The way I hear it, our boy Graden is just about the smartest Negro in all the county and the next one too."

The stubby-eared man whistled as if he were impressed. "Is that a fact?"

I scraped my torn-up old shoes through the gravel and felt

some of the grit and smaller stones come through the holes. I had the idea of running, but that was silly. I had caused this or caused my part in it, at least. And my daddy's part as well. There was nothing to do now but carry it through. I looked down the road for the other cars. They should be here. It would end soon.

My uncle and the other man continued to mock the boy, but I was no longer listening. Finally, I saw headlights come around the bend.

The two other cars pulled up on the roadside. The window of the first car rolled down, and the man beckoned me over. My father was in the seat beside him.

"Is that him?" the driver asked.

I looked at my father, then over my shoulder where my uncle and the other man were questioning the boy. I had to swallow hard before I could speak.

"He says his name is Graden Williams, sir. Said he's on his way up the hill to fetch his brother home from some party."

The driver nodded. "Bring him."

He rolled up his window, and the two cars drove on up the hill slowly. I walked over to the boy and looked at him closely. His dark skin glistened in the glare of the lights. He stared back at me without blinking.

I nodded to my uncle. The other fellow stepped forward.

"Why don't you hop in the car, son. We'll give you a ride up to catch that brother of yours."

"I thank you, sir, but it's a pleasant night. I'd rather walk."

Fear had now taken full grip of the boy. He looked out over the reedy grass, as if searching for help.

The other man reached out for the boy's arm. "Get in the car, boy."

He led Graden towards the open door.

My uncle gave me a tight smile.

"You're doing fine. This ain't easy. It ain't easy for any of us, but you have to trust that what we're doing is right. That boy there is nothing but trouble."

He patted me on the arm and headed towards the car. I stayed behind for a moment, alone. I felt nauseous, but I didn't want to look weak in front of the others or in front of my uncle. I tried to steel myself, but I could only think of what was coming next. I stood almost exactly where the black boy had stood. I looked out over the scrub and grasses, the cracked and random rocks, and the gnarled, old pine tree rising up behind them. And I saw a pair of eyes looking back at me from the tall grass.

23

AMBLAN, 2008

"WHY DIDN'T YOU take me, too?"

Our eyes locked. I looked at Warren, truly looked at him, and realized that I wasn't seeing him for the first time. He had grown old, but his eyes hadn't changed. I knew now why he had come, without police, without media, and why he had never been able to let go of what happened to his brother. And now I also knew that anything I could tell him would be irrelevant. He was a man who had spent almost his entire adult life looking for the people involved in his brother's abduction, and there was no argument that I could make that would persuade him that I was any different from the others. And maybe he was right. My father was a good man, but what category do you assign to a good man who does a horrible thing? He was right. The scales don't balance that way.

"You were there," I said.

"Yeah, I was there. Hiding in the grass. You looked right at me, and you left me there. I want to know why."

He was holding the stock of the rifle in his left hand and rubbing the last drops of melted snow from his greying hair with his right. He paced back and forth in front of the chair, keeping his eyes on me. The picture of his brother lay on the table between us. Then he suddenly leaned forward, his whole body hungry for the answer.

"If I had said something to the others, you would have ended up the same as your brother."

It was the wrong answer. He stopped pacing and lifted the rifle.

"Wait! Wait! Wait! Wait!" I shouted, half-stumbling half-rising from the chair with my hands in the air.

He had the barrel pointed straight at my head. He took deep, heaving breaths but his aim was steady.

"Just wait." I said, moving slowly.

I tried to stay calm, but I could see that he was unpredictable, ready to pull the trigger at the slightest provocation. He had wanted to join his brother in that car, to be brave enough to do something to save him or else die with him. It must have haunted him every day since it had happened, knowing that his brother was taken away while he hid in the long grass beneath the pine tree. He must have wished that he had died then too, and maybe he still wished it now. I could feel the blood beating in my temples, a quick steady pounding.

"Listen, I'll tell you whatever you want. OK? But not with that gun pointed at me. Sit. Sit down."

For a few seconds, he stared at me while I held my breath.

"We'll talk," I continued in what I hoped was a soothing voice. I put my hand on my chest. "But ... I take pills. For my heart. I need them."

He stared at me for a moment longer, then nodded. He lowered himself into the chair, but I could see his finger flexing on the trigger guard.

Keeping my eyes on him, I hauled myself to my feet then shuffled off towards the kitchen.

Once I was there, I turned on the tap and scooped a handful of cool water into my mouth, leaning over the sink and fighting for composure. Warren's agitation was steadily increasing. If I went back into the living room, I had no doubt he would shoot me.

My coat hung tantalizingly in the foyer, but I would have to cross the doorway to the living room to get there. I had another pair of boots and a second, albeit lighter, coat in the mudroom off the back of the kitchen. I could get out that way, but how could I outrun him? Warren must have driven here. If the keys were in his pocket, there was no way to get them. I thought of slashing his tires, but there hadn't been any car in the driveway when I came in, so he must have parked it somewhere else. The only solution I could think of was to stay off the road. If I slipped out the back and through the woods, he'd have to follow on foot. I remembered the shine on his boots and knew they hadn't been waterproofed, and I remembered how he had seemed to favour one leg while getting comfortable in the chair. It wouldn't be easy for me to hike through the woods and over the hill in these conditions, but it would be much more manageable for me than it would be for him.

I opened the cupboard doors above the sink and pulled down a bottle of aspirin. I slammed the doors loudly and rattled the bottle, then slipped into the back room. I put on the jacket and boots and stepped outside. I knew my head start would not be a long one. I ran across the yard as quickly as I could, all the while waiting to hear the back door open, a shot ring out. The jacket was meant for spring, and the wind tore through it mercilessly. The boots held up much better, but the snow was deep, and my legs were already burning after the short dash to the edge of the woods. Once I was under the trees, the snow hadn't collected as heavily, and the going was much easier.

I allowed myself to look back, once. There was no movement coming from the house, but I knew it would not be long. I used the underbrush to pull myself forward, and it didn't take very long for the slope to change from uphill to down. Still, I was sweating by the time I started down the other side, and the combination of wet skin and wind was a dangerous one. I continued at a steady pace, looking occasionally over my shoulder to see if Warren was following.

For a few moments, I even thought of quitting. I considered that maybe Warren deserved his revenge. I had spent my entire adult life thinking of my father, and the sacrifice that he felt he had to make for me. I had given almost no thought to the boy in the chair, tied and bleeding in the centre of that old shed. My uncle had urged me to participate, handing me a pair of blood-rusted pliers. The others were watching closely, judging whether or not I had it in me. The soft northern boy that got picked on in school. I felt the pressure of their eyes on me, had horrific visions of what might be done to me or my father if I didn't step forward, but I was frozen. I choked back vomit, and my legs felt hollowed out beneath me, but I could not look away.

The boy's face was unrecognizable. His clothes had been torn off, and he slumped limp and motionless, other than the occasional gurgle or twitch of his foot. His dark skin absorbed the overhead light, but it was wet with blood. I don't know how long I stared at him before my father took the pliers from my hand and led me out into the night air. He whispered to me, then stepped back inside. I could still see the door closing on him, still remember the screams coming from inside.

Yes, Warren deserved his revenge. And he deserved an answer to the question that had so clearly haunted him ever since that night. But I was a coward then, and a coward now, and so Warren would be twice denied. I carried on.

After about forty-five minutes of hiking, I heard a soft buzzing. There was lots of wildlife in the area, but this was definitely an unnatural sound. I stopped, waited, listened. The buzzing grew louder. It was an engine.

I plunged forward. There would be very few trucks out on a day like this, and I desperately wanted to reach the road before this one passed. I hurled myself through bushes and scrambled over fallen logs, ignoring the dangers of deep trenches and the uneven ground. I could hear my heart pounding as the noise grew closer, then saw the woods open up into a clearing. It was only after I burst out of the woods, frantically waving my arms, that I considered the possibility of it being Warren's truck.

Headlights set the snow aglow as they bounced above the rutted road, then came to a slow stop. The driver was young, maybe in his mid-twenties. I didn't know who he was, though I thought I might have seen him around. He threw the passenger door open.

"You all right, mister?"

I nodded stiffly. The hike over, the cold set in suddenly. My hands and arms were numb, as well as my nose and lips.

"You look like a mess. Get on in. I have a blanket in the back there that you can wrap yourself in. What the hell are you doing out here in that coat?"

I didn't answer, just retrieved the blanket and tucked it around myself as tightly as I could manage. He stared at me for a second, assessing, then reached for his CB radio.

"Hey, it's Roger. I just picked up an old guy at the side of the hill, seems a little disoriented."

The response from the other end was just a haze of static to me.

"Nope, don't know who he is, but he looks like he might be in a bad way. I'm gonna bring him in just as quick as the road lets me."

The young man turned to me.

"Don't be alarmed, mister. I'm just going to check for some ID."

He flipped aside a corner of the blanket and pulled the wallet out of my pocket. He thumbed through it without really looking, keeping his attention on the road. He found a card, glanced at it quickly, then was back on the CB.

"He don't have much on him, but there's a library card, says the fella's name is Earl Daniel."

I had to blow against my lips to get them to part. I huddled inside the blanket, trembling while I answered.

"Olsen," I said. "My name is Earl Olsen."

I tuned out his reply. I rested my head against the window and closed my eyes.

WARREN

24

AMBLAN, 2008

IT TOOK ME A FEW MINUTES to realize that Earl was gone, but he wasn't hard to follow. I tracked his steps to the edge of the woods. From there his footprints were shallower and less distinct, but I moved forward, guided by which branches had the snow brushed off them and which hadn't. Searching was my life. I had found him across decades and miles, and I would find him again across these woods.

I could hear the howl of the wind, but underneath the trees it was calm. The snow was luminescent beneath the three-quarter moon, bright enough that I could easily see the way forward. My knee ached with the uphill grade, and my socks were wet from having trudged through Earl's yard, but the stillness allowed me to focus, one step at a time.

When I faltered, I thought of the night I had lost Graden. I replaced the snow-laden trees with dew-slicked reeds, the rotted, fallen logs with moss-covered rocks, the eerie silence with the cacophony of crickets and toads. The thought of Graden and of all that I owed him allowed me, each time, to take one more step.

When the hill started to flatten, I stopped to rest. I couldn't feel my hands or my feet. The blood pooled in my upper arms, causing them to ache. I felt nauseous, and so I sat down for a moment, my back against the trunk of an evergreen. I removed my gloves and examined my hands. The lines on my palms were white. The skin on my knuckles had cracked and begun to bleed, and my fingers were too stiff to bend. On my right hand, the curled and crippled fingers had turned blue, and the scar running down the length of the hand had split open. My breath was shallow. I tried to check my boots to see whether or not the snow was getting in, but I couldn't work the laces with my fingers. I leaned back and closed my eyes, giving myself permission to rest.

"C'mon," Graden said. "It's time to go home."

He was standing there, just a few feet away from me. I couldn't make him out very well in the swirling snow, but it was him. I laughed just at hearing his voice again. The snow cleared for a moment, and I could see him distinctly now, standing in front of the old grain shed.

"It's time to go home."

I downed my gin and said a loud farewell to the half-dozen others who were gathered there. I patted John Young on the back, blew a kiss to Faye. I stumbled out the door, leaning on my brother as we walked.

"You know I wish you wouldn't come to this place."

"And you know I don't need you to lecture me," I slurred.

I took my arm off his shoulder, teetered, then straightened and continued on alone. Graden trailed a few steps behind. When we reached the old pine, I stopped.

"Gotta piss," I called out over my shoulder.

I waded through the tall grass towards the tree, placed my right hand on it to steady myself, undid my pants, and released a stream of urine against the base. I wavered in my relief, then pulled my pants back up.

I knew what was coming next — the sound of a car engine, the headlights punching two holes in the darkness, the men in the black cars taking my brother away while I hid by the tree, trying unsuccessfully to will myself to move forward, to do something, anything. I felt dizzy and light-headed. My vision blurred, and my thoughts turned sluggish.

I was on the porch beside my father, who was drunk, smoking cigarettes, and warning me about challenging whites. I was seated beside Graden on the bus going to Jackson, listening to hymns sung out in strong, clear voices. I was crouching in the grass beneath the pine tree, head swimming with gin. I was resting with my back against an evergreen behind Earl's house with my boots and gloves removed, feeling the sharp, cold stab of snow down the back of my coat.

Shivering, I tried to stand up so I could warn Graden about the men who were coming, but I found I couldn't budge. A short distance away my brother stood patiently, waiting for me to join him on the walk home.

"I'm gonna go on ahead," he called. "You come when you're ready."

He shone that smile at me, and I felt as if the sun had risen inside my chest. I wasn't cold any more. I didn't worry about the cars coming around the bend or the men smiling on the courthouse steps. I no longer had to remember him as the torn-up body in the coroner's photo. He was here and he was whole, and I knew that they could no longer touch him.

"Wait," I called out. "I'm coming."

I tried to make it to my feet, but the snow was soft and deep, and I stumbled, falling forward on to my hands and knees. And so I began crawling towards him like I had on that New Year's Day so long ago, when everything was buried in white, and the world seemed fresh and bright and ready to begin anew. I tried to tell him how sorry I was. How much I loved him and missed him. I could see him just a few feet ahead, where he had stopped once again to wait for me.

"You shouldn't have come to get me," I said.

His smile was a light, pushing away the darkness.

"I wouldn't leave without you," he said. "Come on. It's time to go."

He reached out his hand to me and hauled me up so that I was finally standing beside him. Then we turned to walk home.

25

AMBLAN, 2008

WHEN WE GOT TO the hospital, I told them my name was Earl Olsen, but the doctor recognized me and had the nurse correct the information on my sheet. They kept me overnight to treat mild hypothermia and released me in the morning.

Two weeks passed before Warren's body was found. The tracks he'd left were long since covered over, and the rifle was lying in the snow a few feet away from him. Just another hunter who lost his way. Not unusual in these parts.

I wasn't happy to know he was gone, but I wasn't sad about it either. I wished I could say different, but the truth was it didn't affect me much at all to hear about it. My only sympathy was for the young man hiding by the old pine tree, staring out from the darkness, too frightened to act. That was who Warren Williams really was. His whole life after that was just the consequence.

A few reporters from down in the States poked around for a bit, but they didn't stay long or pry hard, and the folks up here tend to be pretty tight-lipped around strangers anyway.

About a week after he was discovered, I saw an interview with his sister. There was a postcard in his pocket that she had sent him years ago, the only personal effect they found on him. She was on the front steps of her house in Philadelphia, dressed simply in a plain brown skirt and a white blouse, her hair done up in a bun. The reporter was off-camera.

"Is there a reason he was in Amblan?"

She hesitated before answering, looking deliberately into the camera. I waited to hear my name, and I was OK with it. After waking in the hospital I had gone back to using Earl Daniel, but if the police came for me, I wouldn't deny it. I'd done that for too long. Every man is convinced of his own innocence. It takes someone else to show him otherwise. I looked at the screen, and Etta seemed to look out of it, right at me.

"Probably not. No. Warren moved around a lot. There isn't anywhere that he'd turn up that I'd say is surprising."

I wasn't sure if I was relieved by her answer or not.

"Warren dedicated his later years to bringing your younger brother's killers to justice. Did he find peace in that?"

"Well, peace isn't something Warren had a relationship with. He was always too hard on himself. I hope it gave him some comfort, though."

"How do you want your brother to be remembered?"

She paused to think. I watched her draw herself together, her poise apparent even on the screen.

"I want him to be remembered for what he was. A good man. A dedicated man. One with flaws, certainly, just like anyone else, but a man who set his mind to something and wouldn't let anyone deter him from it. I know he got a lot of mail from folks who just wanted him to stop stirring things up, but he believed that what he was doing was right, and he had the courage to keep doing it. That's one thing that both my brothers had in common, Graden and Warren. They were both brave men."

ACKNOWLEDGEMENTS

I would like to thank the following people and organizations for their role in this process:

The School for Writers at Humber College for its dedication to supporting and developing new writers and, in particular, Joan Barfoot for her invaluable advice and guidance.

Margaret Hart, formerly of the HSW Literary Agency, who was tireless in her efforts on my behalf. I could not have asked for a better representative.

All the staff at TAP Books and Dundurn for their support, including those who work behind the scenes.

A special thank you to my editor, Diane Young, for her patient and thoughtful treatment of the material. Your insight has greatly strengthened the work.

And finally to Jim Holling, Jan Metcalfe, Brian Henry, Emily Donaldson, and Christine Walde for having read prior manuscripts and offered helpful advice, and to my friends and family for their support.

NOTE

I have tried to avoid writing a history book, and so in this story I have only tangentially touched on the struggle to mobilize black voters that took place in rural Mississippi in the early sixties. Although the Freedom Summer efforts of 1964 are the best known, local organizers had been working on similar voter registration projects for years before then. The imported students and the local volunteers risked everything during that time to change Mississippi, and the world. Their courage and sacrifice are inspiring and, in some cases, unimaginable. For more information about Freedom Summer and the projects that preceded it, I recommend consulting the Mississippi Department of Archives and History (http://mdah.state.ms.us) or www.freedom50.org.